THE GIRLS OF CANBY HALL

7 | 7

Four Is a Crowd

Emily Chase

D1026028

SCHOLASTIC INC.
New York Toronto London Auckland Sydney Tokyo

ISBN 0-590-33248-1

12 11 10 9 8 7 6 5 4 3 2 1   10   4 5 6 7 8 9/8

Printed in the U. S. A.   06

Four Is a Crowd

7 THE GIRLS OF CANBY HALL 7

Roommates
Our Roommate is Missing
You're No Friend of Mine
Keeping Secrets
Summer Blues
Best Friends Forever
Four is a Crowd

CHAPTER ONE

Dana Morrison climbed out of the van that had picked her up at the Greenleaf, Massachusetts, train station and brought her out to Canby Hall for her second year at boarding school.

She stretched her legs and shook her long brown hair off the back of her neck. The calendar might say September 5, but it was hot as the dog days of summer. It had been so steamy in the back of the van that Dana felt like a pizza being delivered.

She fantasized about a tall glass of the great lemonade that Mr. Fiorello made at the Tutti Frutti ice cream parlor in town. Then she imagined how terrific it would feel to dive into Hudson's creek. Maybe later. First she had to get all this stuff up to her room.

She looked around. There were parents and girls everywhere, unloading out of cars suitcases and trunks and cartons and bicycles and tennis rackets and stuffed animals, and

1

lugging them up the stairs of Canby Hall's three dorms — Addison, Baker, and Charles. The heat was slowing the action to a crawl. Dana thought that from a plane, the campus would look just like an ant farm.

She wished her mother and younger sister Maggie could have driven her up. But Maggie was already back in school, and her mother had to work. She was a New York City department store fashion buyer, and fall was one of her busiest times. Dana's dad was off working in Hawaii for a year. He had just married his new wife, Eve. This put an end to all the hopes Dana had had for her parents getting back together. She sighed at the thought of this, and picked up two of her suitcases.

When she got up to her old room — 407 Baker — she gasped. While they'd been gone over the summer, aliens from outer space had come in and painted. That was the only possible explanation for the color. All last year, the room had been painted what Dana's roommate Faith called Insane Asylum Green. Now, though, it was a bright electric peacock blue. Dana stood in the doorway for a moment, trying to talk herself into the color.

It was hopeless. She couldn't. At least with Insane Asylum Green, you kind of stopped noticing it after a while. There was no way you could stop noticing this. Ever. It was a color you usually only had to see on parade floats, or in the costumes of ladies sitting on top of elephants in the circus.

"Gadzooks!" she heard someone shout behind her. She turned to find her roommate Faith. They hugged each other hello, while at the same time collapsing in laughter at the awfulness of the color.

"It's really incredibly, unbelievably horrible, isn't it?" Dana said to Faith.

"No," Faith said and paused. "It's worse than that."

"What are we going to do?"

"I don't know. We'd better wait for Shelley and have a pow-wow." Shelley was their third roommate, who would be coming in from Iowa sometime that day.

Dana went down and helped Faith haul her stuff up. It turned out she had taken the same train up as Dana. But Faith had boarded in Washington, D.C. and gotten into a different car and so they hadn't discovered each other. Then Faith slept through the Greenleaf stop and didn't wake up until just before the next one.

"I blew my whole first week's allowance on the cab," Faith said. "But what was I going to do?"

"Nobody could drive you up?" Dana asked.

"No. Mom had to be in court today. Sarah's already started her classes at Georgetown. Richard, well he's only fourteen — and short for his age. He wanted to drive me, but Mom would've had to put blocks on the pedals so he could reach them."

Faith's mother was a social worker, the sole support of the family since Faith's dad, a cop, was killed trying to stop a robbery.

"You look really good," Dana said. "A little too skinny, but that's not too bad, considering how sick you were over the summer." She was referring to the mysterious virus that had put Faith in the hospital in August.

"Yeah, there's about ten pounds less of me," Faith said, pulling at the waistband of her jeans to show how loose it was. "But they tell me I'll live."

"I'm glad," Dana said. "If you'd died, they might've moved Agatha Pumphrey in here." Agatha had the surliest disposition at Canby Hall. She had gone through seven roommates before the school finally just gave her a private room.

Faith grinned and messed up Dana's hair. She knew the joke was Dana's way of saying she cared. Both of them used jokes a lot in place of things that were too hard to say. It was only one of so many ways they were alike. They were also both independent, smart, and interested in figuring everything out — ideas, people, life. They almost always agreed on these big sorts of things, and on smaller stuff like music and movies, too.

When they had first come to Canby Hall a year ago, this rapport had surprised them both. Faith was black and had not had any white friends back in D.C. Dana was white and hadn't had any black friends in New York. And so it was kind of amazing to both of them that they turned out so much alike.

When they got the last of Faith's stuff up to the room, Dana surveyed the mess and said, "I guess we'd better start putting this all away. Pretty soon Shelley'll be here with all *her* stuff and then it'll be impossible to move, let alone unpack!"

As they worked, they talked about the trip they had taken over the summer out to Pine Bluff, Iowa, to visit Shelley and her family. And about Faith getting so sick and having to be flown home. And about what Dana had been doing the past month in New York, besides sending Faith joke get-well cards. And what Faith had been doing while she recuperated.

"I think Richard and I must've played about six hundred games of Scrabble. Having to stay in for so long just about drove me nuts. About the only good part about being a tragic invalid was that Johnny came down for an emergency weekend visit."

Johnny Bates was Faith's boyfriend. He lived in Greenleaf and went to the local high school. She was crazy about him, although she tried to seem cool about it. Being cool was important to Faith.

"How'd it go?" Dana asked her. "Did your family fall in love with him?"

"Well, you know they all met him when they came up to get me in July, so it wasn't like he was a total stranger. Sarah thinks he's adorable. She says he gives her ideas about robbing the cradle. Richard thinks anyone who'll play Frisbee with him every day is about as neat as Luke Skywalker. My mother —

well, I think she thinks Johnny's fine, but she's also nervous that I'm in love. I'm sixteen and all, but I guess no matter how old you are, when it happens, it's a shock to parents. It means you're growing up, and they have to deal with that. You just have to give them time to adjust. Did you see Randy?"

Dana's new romance, which had started during the summer intensives, was with a local country boy named Randy Crowell.

"No, summer's the busiest time for his family. They have to tend the orchards and get up enough hay to carry the horses through the winter. I'm not sure how this is going to turn out. He and I are completely different. It's probably not going to last forever, but I'm having a good time now. He sent me some letters while I was home. They're real sensitive. I'll show you some."

"Just censor the mushier parts, will you?" Faith asked. "You know I've got a pretty low tolerance for romantic goo." She stretched as she said this, trying to put the last of her books on the highest shelf above her desk. She was even taller than Dana. She was hoping that before she stopped growing, she'd hit six feet.

"Faith Thompson, hard as nails," Dana mocked. "You don't fool me for a minute with that front. I'd like to eavesdrop on some of those conversations you and Johnny have out there in the ash grove."

"I talk about photography and he talks about computers."

"I'll bet," Dana said.

Faith just turned and smiled.

"Yikes!" they both heard from the doorway. They looked and there was Shelley Hyde. "Where are my sunglasses?" she said.

"We know, we know," Faith said, and ran over to give her roommate a welcome-back hug.

"It is so incredibly, amazingly, unbelievably, atrociously awful, isn't it?" Shelley said. The three of them hugged and laughed and ultimately fell down together in the middle of the floor.

"What are we going to do about it, though?" Shelley asked, rolling onto her back, scanning the room, squinting for dramatic effect. She had become interested in drama at Canby Hall, and in the process, had picked up sweeping gestures and some voice affectations. When she went too far with this, Faith and Dana teased her out of it, calling her the Meryl Streep of Canby Hall.

"We were hoping *you'd* tell us," Faith said.

"Well, for sure we're going to have to do a custom paint job here."

"But what color?" Dana asked. "A softer blue maybe?"

"What about a kind of sand color?" Faith wondered.

"Black," Shelley said.

"Black!?" Dana said.

"Excuse me, I must have something wrong," Faith said. "I thought I heard you say black."

"Why not?" Shelley said. "It'd be dramatic."

"Even more dramatic," Faith said, ruffling up her short Afro with her fingers, "will be the speed with which her highness, our beloved headmistress, throws us out of this school."

"Oh, come on, Faith," Shelley argued. "When has Patrice Allardyce ever passed through the lowly halls of Baker House?"

"But what about Alison?" Dana wondered. Alison Cavanaugh might be the hippest housemother east of the Alleghenies, and a good friend of Dana's, but even *she* would probably have some reservations about having a room in her dorm that looked like a bat cave.

"Well, all I've got to say is that a school that gives girls a room *this* color," Shelley gestured with a large wave of her hand, "doesn't have much right to stop poor students from making it liveable again."

"You've got a point there, girl," Faith mused.

"I wonder how many cans we'll need?" Dana said.

A few hours later, they had gotten everything put away and were lying around, talking with Shelley about what had happened in Pine Bluff after they left. Shelley was still seeing her old boyfriend Paul back there, but was also now in heavy like (just short of love) with Tom, who lived here and went to school with Johnny Bates.

"Well," Shelley said with a shake of her

head that tossed her curly blonde hair. It had grown longer over the summer and now had a mildly wild look. She also had a great tan from two months outdoors. "It was nice being with Paul again. We do much better in person than in letters. But I missed Tom like crazy. You know he called long distance *five* times!"

Shelley had gone through a lot of changes in her first year at Canby Hall. When she arrived, she was Paul's girl and her parents' girl, and was sure she was going to marry him and be exactly like them. Now she had two boyfriends and was intent on becoming an actress and starting acting workshop in New York when she graduated.

Shelley now unpacked a special cake her mother had baked for Faith.

"To put some meat on those bones," Shelley said, taking the foil off. "Your favorite — spice cake with cream cheese frosting."

Faith dipped a finger in the icing.

"No sense standing on ceremony. Nobody in this room's going to get written up in any etiquette book. Mmmmm. Good. I might even give you two a piece when I'm done." But even as she was saying this, she was getting out a knife and cutting huge hunks for them.

The three roommates ate the cake and speculated on what junior year was going to be like, what classes they were taking, how different it was coming back today from that day a year ago when they had all arrived — green, new, terrified, transfer sophomores.

"Now we're sophisticated upperclass-women!" Shelley said.

"Yeah," Faith said, "but some of that ignorance was bliss. Remember, back then we didn't know anything about the food in the cafeteria."

"Ohhh, don't remind me," Shelley groaned. "How will I be able to go back down there after two months of my mother's deeelicious home cooking?"

"Yes," Dana teased. "We can see it was delicious."

"I did gain a little, didn't I?" Shelley said, tugging her slightly tight t-shirt down over her hips. "I'm still down at least ten pounds, though, from the little tub of lard I was when I got here last year."

"I didn't even notice your lard," Faith said. "I was too whim-whammed by how weird you acted when you saw that your new room-mate was black!"

"I did *not* act weird!" Shelley insisted. "You just thought I did!"

"Come on you two. I don't want to recreate that memorable scene — *or* that week of silence that followed it. I'm just happy it all worked out between us, that we're the three best friends at Canby Hall, and that nothing's going to change that."

"Right on," Faith said, then got up. "I don't know about you two, but there's no way I can face whatever they've cooked down there in Hell's Kitchen. What do you say we have a nutritionally corrupt dinner of banana splits over at the old Tutti Frutti? It'll be one hot walk into town, but once we get inside, it'll be air-conditioned bliss." She went over and looked out the window, which looked down on the drive in front of Baker.

"Holy cow!" she said, and let out a long, low whistle. "Will you look at what just arrived at Canby Hall!"

CHAPTER TWO

Shelley and Dana rushed over to join Faith at the window. They didn't have to ask what she was looking at.

Parked in front of the main entrance to Baker House was a shiny navy blue limousine. Behind it was a matching blue Cadillac. Two uniformed chauffeurs were unloading the two cars.

"Look at that!" Shelley fairly gasped. At that moment, one of the chauffeurs was pulling a large color tv from the trunk of the Cadillac. On the sidewalk next to the car were a video-recorder and the components of an expensive-looking stereo. There were also skis, four tennis rackets in presses, and an electric typewriter.

"I count seven of those baby blue trunks," Faith said.

"Nine baby blue suitcases," Dana added.

"Who *is* this chick?" Faith wondered.

"And why didn't I get her for *my* roommate?" Dana said. Two sets of eyes glared at her. "Only kidding," she said. "But really, whose stuff is this? Nobody we know — unless somebody's father made a killing in the market over the summer."

"Even if my dad made a killing in the market," Shelley said, "he wouldn't be spending it on navy blue limousines and baby blue luggage for me."

"She's right. This is not standard style — even for rich folks," Faith said. "May I point out the California plates on the limo?"

Suddenly, a willowy blonde girl in white pants and a black new wave shirt came out of Baker and started giving orders.

"Okay boys, the good news is that we're the last ones to arrive, so you won't have to fight the crowds getting in. The bad news is that I'm on the third floor and there's no elevator. Have you got everything out of the car?"

"Yes, Miss Young," one of the chauffeurs said.

"Good, then I'll take off and find someplace in town to get dinner, while you get this stuff upstairs and Nanette puts it away."

"I have it here," the maid said, checking a notebook she pulled from her pocket, "that there's a dining hall of some sort on the campus."

"Yeah," the girl said, tossing her hair with a shake of her head. "I walked by and saw *what* sort. It's impossible. I'll have to find someplace in town to eat."

"But your mother wants you to have the

experience of this place," the maid chastised.

"Well, I'll start getting into it tomorrow. It's my last night with wheels. I can't believe this prison doesn't let anyone have a car. How am I going to exist without my little Jaguar? What do you suppose they do around here — walk?!"

She slid behind the wheel of the Cadillac and started it up.

"Oh Nanette," the girl said, sticking her head out the open car window, "when you get up there, you'll see there are a couple of other girls in the room. Apparently they actually put three girls in some rooms here. That just wouldn't be possible for me, of course. Could you talk to someone and see if you can get me a private room? If there's any problem, call mother and have her arrange it."

"Yes, Miss Pamela," the maid said and set off into the dorm. Miss Pamela threw the Cadillac into gear and screeched out down the driveway at about forty.

The three roommates turned to look at each other.

"Miss Pamela wants a private room," Shelley said.

"I hope she gets it," Dana said. "Can you imagine living with *her*?"

"Wait a minute," Faith teased, "I thought you were the one who wanted to move in with her."

"No, I'm the one who wanted to move in with her color tv. I *am* dying to know who she is, though. Somebody must know something by now."

As if on cue, Casey Flint walked in. Casey was the most well-informed girl at Canby Hall — not about geometry or biology or English, but about who was going with whom, who was on social probation, who was in trouble for keeping a secret puppy in her room.

"Casey!" they all shouted at once. They hadn't seen their friend since the end of summer intensives. They all wanted to know about her trip with her parents.

"Oh *that*," she said dismissively. "That can wait. It pales before the juicy tidbit I bring you now."

"It isn't that you happen to know who the mystery girl is?" Dana nodded casually toward the open window. "We've just been watching Cleopatra's entrance into Rome."

"Except this Cleo's not from ancient Egypt," Casey said.

"Yes," Shelley said. "I noticed the California license plates." All this nonchalance was part of the Canby Hall gossip game. Even though Casey was dying to tell and the others were dying to know, everyone had to pretend to be very cool about it.

"If you noticed the plates," Casey went on, "you might have got to wondering if Miss Mega-Rich could possibly come our way from the southern part of that state, the Los Angeles area, more precisely — Hollywood, home of the stars." Casey was playing this one for everything it was worth.

"Case," Faith said. "Spit it out, will you?" Faith was easily bored with this kind of fooling around. She figured that if you had something to say, you should say it.

"Okay, okay," Casey said. "Well, my dears, it seems that Canby Hall's newest junior transfer is Pamela Young, troubled and troublemaking daughter of one of America's queens of the silver screen. . . ."

"Yvonne Young!" Shelley yelled.

"You're kidding," Dana said. Faith just gave out with a long, low whistle. All three of them were impressed. Yvonne Young was one of the top actresses in all of film.

"Cindy Fletcher knew Pamela a little out there," Casey went on. "They went to private school together. Cindy says Pamela's a real spoiled brat."

"Everyone always says that about rich kids," Dana said. "Maybe she's okay."

"I'll bet she knows all the big celebs," Shelley said. "All those stars hang out with each other, because everyone else just goes gaga over them. They hide out at the Malibu Colony and have Chinese food delivered in so they won't get mobbed at a restaurant."

Everyone looked at Shelley in amazement.

"Just how do you come by all this inside information in the middle of Iowa?" Faith asked, teasing.

"Believe it or not," Shelley said sarcastically, "even though we're out there in the cornfields, they still sell *People* magazine." She hated when her city friends acted like she was a hick.

"Cindy Fletcher says Pamela's been tossed out of three or four other schools," Casey went on. "Apparently Yvonne's shipping her out here to get her away from the bright lights and bad influences. Out here to the simple life we live in the woods."

"Well, it *might* be simpler for her here," Shelley said, "that is, if everyone restrains herself from making a big fuss over her just because she's the daughter of a big movie star. I think that's what we should try to do — just hang loose and act like she's just another Canby girl to us, that we could care less what her mother does for a living. And that'll make her so relaxed and comfortable that she'll consider us her best friends, and invite us all back home for Thanksgiving. Her mother will fly us out in their private jet and throw a huge party for us so we can meet some of the gang she hangs out with — Robert Redford and Joan Collins and Richard Gere and John Travolta."

Faith looked at Shelley in amazement.

"You are a wonder. There is no one who can work up a bigger fantasy in less time than you. You probably already know the flight time of the jet."

Everyone laughed, including Shelley.

"Hey," Dana said. "I say Pamela Young can wait. What we need more than a trip to Hollywood — at least at this very moment — is a trip to the Tutti Frutti. Robert Redford will have to wait until Thanksgiving to meet me anyway, and right now I need a banana split more than anything else in the world."

"I'll second that," Casey said. "And I know what I'm talking about. I'm the only one who has been downstairs and seen what they're serving for dinner tonight in the world-renowned Canby Hall dining room."

"What is it?" Dana asked. "I can take it."

"I can't," Faith said.

"An old favorite of everyone's — broiled moccasin."

This dish was actually called London broil, but Casey had renamed it last year in honor of its leathery texture. Faith said that in her family, they would call it "sole food."

"Well, if we're going to go over to Tutti Frutti, we'd better get started. In this heat, the place'll be mobbed. We'll be lucky to get a seat."

On the way back to campus — full of banana splits and cherry sodas and lemonade, and full of stories about their vacations, the four of them were too excited to go straight back to the dorm. They wanted to stay out in what was probably going to be one of the last great nights of summer.

They decided it would be fun to take a walk around the whole campus, which they loved for its beauty and for its history, which they were beginning to feel part of.

Canby Hall had been founded in 1897 by

a wealthy industrialist, Horace Canby, in memory of his little girl, Julia, who had died of fever. In tribute to his lost child, he established a girls' school on the property that would have been her inheritance.

Now there were two-hundred-fifty girls at Canby Hall, but back in the beginning, there had been only thirty. Now there were many buildings. Back in 1897, there had only been Main Building for classes and Baker for living quarters.

They walked past the library, and the science building, which had been added in the early 1900s. The tennis courts and sports center with its indoor and outdoor pools were even more recent additions to the campus.

But some of Canby Hall was exactly the same as it had been when the school opened. The chapel, farm, and stables were still there, as were the skating pond and wooded paths and picnic areas. The Canby family home was now the house of the headmistress, Patrice Allardyce.

Most Canby girls were at least mildly terrified by P.A., as she was called by everyone — behind her back, that is. She ran the school with an iron hand, tolerated no bad behavior, or bad manners. Being even five minutes late for curfew could get a girl grounded.

P.A. was mistress of the withering look. Girls had been known to break down into tears under one of these. She was tall and imposing in her blonde, frosty way, and when she arched one of her eyebrows, it was hard for a girl to hold onto her composure.

Almost everyone respected P.A. Some girls also admired her. Faith was one of them.

"That is one cool lady," she would say, and give a heavy nod of appreciation.

The lights were on in P.A.'s house tonight as the four of them walked by it.

"Well," Dana said, "they may be letting movie star kids into Canby Hall, and we may have made it into the lofty ranks of the upperclasswomen, and they may even install a French chef in the dining hall, but here's one thing that'll remain unchanged for all the time we're here — good old P.A. sitting in that armchair in her living room at night, sipping her tea, and storing up her energy for another day of terrorizing us."

And sure enough, there she was, sitting in her armchair, sipping her tea, just as Dana had predicted. They all looked in as they walked by.

Suddenly, though, P.A. jumped out of her seat. Her teacup went crashing to the floor. They were too far away to hear it shatter, but close enough to see her go over and stand facing the fireplace, resting her head on the mantle. Then she turned and was clearly shouting at someone in the room. Or, if not shouting, talking in an animated, disturbed way. Whoever it was in there with her had clearly caused her to lose the P.A. cool in a major way.

"Sssh," Shelley said, although no one had

said anything. They stood there stock still and waited and watched, as a handsome young guy with long blond hair walked across the space framed by the front window, and went over and pulled P.A. — who, from the shaking of her shoulders, appeared to now be crying — into his arms, then held her there, patting her back comfortingly.

"We'd better get out of here," Dana said to the rest of them. "I've got a feeling P.A. would not be crazy about us seeing this."

"Whatever *this* is," Faith added.

"Wow!" Shelley said as she ran after them. "A movie star's daughter in Baker. A blond hunk in P.A.'s house. This is going to be some term!"

CHAPTER THREE

Shelley always woke up before her roommates. Morning was her favorite part of the day. She liked being awake while everything was still quiet. The other thing she liked about morning was breakfast — her favorite meal of the day.

She brought her French text down with her to the cafeteria. French was her absolute worst subject and she wanted to get a jump on it this term. She usually took a table by the long, leaded glass windows so that the thin morning sunlight would fall across the pages of her notebooks. Studying like this was such a peaceful way to start the day.

Today, though, when she came out of the cafeteria line with her usual tray of pancakes and scrambled eggs and orange juice and milk, she stopped midway to the windows — like a deer in the forest that has heard a new noise.

What stopped her was Pamela Young, who was sitting in the middle of the dining room, drinking coffee and reading a paper. Shelley wouldn't have expected Pamela Young to be an early riser. She thought everyone in Hollywood slept until noon with their eyeshades on.

Shelley was, of course, dying to meet her. But she didn't want to seem like a goon. The dining room was nearly empty. The few girls who were there had tables to themselves. The only reason to share with someone would be to talk to them. She didn't want to barge in and seem like a stupid fan or something.

On the other hand, maybe Pamela was dying for company, and Shelley could be the early bird that got the worm.

She decided it was worth a try.

"Hi," she said in her brightest voice when she got to Pamela's table. "Mind if I sit here?"

Pamela looked up from her paper and focused on Shelley with a stare that was completely devoid of interest.

"Just so you're quiet. I'm really rattled this morning. I've been up since dawn, nearly *deafened* by all the dreadful wildlife around here. Crickets. Croaking frogs. Birds by the billions. I've got a headache like someone dropped an anvil on me. So if you could keep it down, honey."

With this she went back to her paper.

Shelley took her plate and silver off her tray and tried to put everything on the table silently. She sat down and began eating quickly. All she wanted to do now was get out of here. She felt stupid for having come over and barged in.

As she ate, she took quick looks at Pamela. She sure didn't look like the typical Canby girl. Her blonde hair was long and smooth. The front was a sweep of an even lighter blonde. She was wearing quite a bit of make-up, but so perfectly applied that it seemed almost natural. Her nails were long and polished a bright red. She was wearing a black silk shirt with the short sleeves rolled up. On one arm, she was wearing about ten thin silver bracelets. On the other wrist was a big old man's watch with a brown leather strap.

Canby Hall was not a silk shirt and silver bracelet kind of place. Campus fashions were much more casual — polo shirts and cotton slacks in summer, Oxford cloth shirts and Fair Isle sweaters and jeans and corduroys in winter. And although there were rich girls and poor ones at Canby Hall, they all dressed pretty much the same. If anything, the rich ones, being mostly from staid old New England families who despised showiness, dressed the plainest of all. Pamela Young was going to stick out like a sore — if beautiful — thumb.

Shelley tried to read upside down to see what newspaper Pamela was reading. *M* it said upside down. That meant *W* right side up. It was a fashion paper.

"Do you enjoy the challenge of reading upside down? Or is that how they do it in your country? Or do you want to borrow my paper?" Pamela said sarcastically, pushing the paper across the table at Shelley.

"It's just a trendy little rag," she said. "But I like to make a pass at keeping up with what's going on in the New York fashion scene, don't you?"

"I don't know," Shelley said, thinking fast. "I mostly just keep an eye on what's happening in Paris."

Pamela looked at Shelley for the first time as if she might have possibilities. She picked up a white leather knapsack from the floor and pulled a pack of cigarettes out of the side pocket. She looked around.

"I don't see any ashtrays," she said. "Did I wind up in the non-smoking section?"

"Oh," Shelley said. "I guess the whole school is a non-smoking section. I mean, they don't allow it here. I think some of the girls sneak one now and then. Sometimes you can smell it in the john. But mostly everybody just thinks it's dumb."

At first Pamela didn't say anything, then stuffed the pack back in the pocket of her knapsack, and looked at Shelley as if she were hopeless.

"Well," she said. "I guess you're all going to be very healthy little old ladies, aren't you? Me, I don't think I'm going to live long. The way I drive, I'll probably go out like James Dean — wrapping my Jaguar around a tree.

Not here, of course. Here I'm told we aren't allowed to have anything as necessary as cars."

"Well," Shelley said. "Everything's pretty close by around here. You probably won't miss it all that much. We just walk everywhere."

"I don't walk *anywhere*. In California, *nobody* walks anywhere."

"You're from California?" Shelley asked, playing dumb.

"Topanga Canyon."

"That's near Hollywood, right?" Shelley bluffed, trying to get Pamela to continue.

"Right," Pamela said.

"That's where a lot of the big stars live, isn't it?" Shelley pushed a little more.

"I guess," Pamela said.

"You ever run into anybody famous, like in the supermarket?" Shelley had a feeling that Pamela was not going to be able to resist spilling the beans much longer.

"Welllll," Pamela said, coyly, "Sometimes I run into them in my very own kitchen. My mother knows a lot of them. She does a little acting herself."

"Oh yeah?" Shelley said. "So do I. What's your mom's name? Maybe I've heard of her."

"Yvonne Young," Pamela said, then waited, as if she expected Shelley to faint away under the table. Instead Shelley just said in her coolest voice, "Oh yes, I know her. I saw one of her old pictures on TV a couple of weeks ago at home. The one where she's a ballerina and some admirer sends orchids to her dressing room. And she gets this rare tropical fever from them. And then she falls in love with the doctor who's trying to find a cure for her."

Pamela gave her review of this film by sticking her finger down her throat and pantomiming throwing up.

"*Sands of Time*," Pamela said. "That was the drippiest picture Yvonne ever made."

Pamela thought a minute, then added, "Except for *Rush to Heaven*. That was worse."

"Is that the one where she played the angel who came down to earth to help Clint Eastwood, who was the father of the seven kids and the mother had died? And then the angel fell in love with him and wanted to stay on earth?"

"That's the turkey all right," Pamela said.

"You're right," Shelley said. "It stunk."

They both laughed.

"So," Shelley said. "What's she like — your mother?"

"Yvonne? She's a jerk. She keeps sending me to schools like this."

Shelley was taken aback. Almost no one she knew would call her mother a jerk. Not like this. It took her a moment to recover and find a different conversational line of attack.

"But it must be kind of neat — being the kid of someone famous?"

"Sometimes." Pamela sounded bored. "But mostly it's just a drag. We can't even go shopping for groceries. We just get mobbed by the time we get to the frozen foods section."

"Gross," Shelley said, secretly fantasizing herself as a big star, being mobbed in the supermarket.

"Well, it's not all that bad. We shop for clothes on Rodeo Drive. Everyone else there is a star, too. Or so rich they look down their noses at stars. For movies, we go to private screenings. Yvonne's limo has tinted glass so no one can see it's us inside. And of course, some parts of being a star's daughter are absolutely terrific."

"Like?"

"Like meeting the cutest guys in the world."

"Who?" Shelley said, trying to hide her excitement.

"Oh, I don't know. Matt Dillon. Tom Cruise. Michael Jackson."

"Don't let my roommate know. She's loony about Michael Jackson. If she found out you know him, she'd attach herself to your ankle, to be sure and be around if you run into him."

"That's a problem I run into a lot," Pamela sighed wearily. "People who want to be around me because of who I know. I have to choose my friends very carefully."

At this point, Faith came up to the table. They had planned on bike riding that morning, and Faith was ready to go.

"You done eating?" she asked Shelley.

Pamela looked over and apparently took Faith for a bus girl. She waved a hand at Shelley's dishes and her own half cup of black coffee and said, "Go ahead. You can clear them away. We're done."

Faith's eyes, which had been half shut with sleep, now opened very wide as she glared at Pamela with a look that — well, if looks could kill, Pamela would be a dead girl. And then Faith turned on her heel and stalked out of the cafeteria.

"Boy," Pamela said. "And I thought we had trouble with servants in California."

"That wasn't any servant," Shelley said, jumping up. "That was my roommate!"

"Oh," Pamela said, not sounding particularly sorry, "well, I suppose she must be used to people making that mistake."

"I've got to go now," Shelley said, too flustered and upset to deal with Pamela. She ran after Faith.

She caught up with her on the stairs.

"Hey!" she shouted, out of breath from taking two flights two steps at a time. She grabbed Faith's arm and turned her around. "Stop. Talk to me."

But Faith couldn't. Her face was tight with rage.

"Come on," Shelley pleaded. "So she's a jerk. She'll get straightened out here. Nobody around this place is going to let her get away with that kind of stuff."

"What'd you say to her after I left?" Faith asked.

Suddenly, Shelley realized that she should have stood up for her roommate, that she should have told Pamela how awful she was. That was what Faith wanted to hear now.

"I told her she'd better watch what she says around here, that maybe back in California she's a big deal, but here she's just a new transfer and if she wants to make any friends she'd better get nice fast!"

"Boy, you really told her good," Faith said, breaking into a smile.

"Oh, you bet I did," Shelley said, now really getting into her lie. "And then I told her that if she ever offended my roommate again, I'd punch her out."

"You did?" Faith said, amazed and happy. "You really told her that?"

"Well, I was plenty mad."

Faith gave her a squeeze on the shoulder. "I can't tell you how great it makes me feel to hear this."

And I can't tell you what a crumb I feel like, lying to you like this, Shelley thought. At least she *wished* she had said all those things. Maybe that counted for something. Or *did* she really wish she had? That would mean insulting Pamela Young, and as stuck-up and obnoxious as she had seemed, there was still a real pull of glamour about her.

Shelley was just too mixed up to think about it anymore right then.

CHAPTER FOUR

"Oooooweee!" Casey shouted, coming through the door of 407 late on Saturday afternoon. "I'd better go back and get my miner's hat with the light on it. Where did you three get this brilliant idea — out of *Better Homes and Tunnels*?"

Faith, Dana, and Shelley were nearly done painting their room completely black. Casey's was the first outside opinion they'd gotten.

"Dramatic though, don't you think?" Dana prompted from the top of a ladder in the corner. She had been going back and forth on this decision all day. She swung between thinking it was going to look incredibly sharp, and thinking it was going to look like the Black Hole of Calcutta.

"I guess," Casey said, but she sounded dubious. "Aren't you worried that you'll get — well, depressed — in here?"

"I think it'll be like we're in our own cozy cave," Shelley said. She was on the floor,

31

painting carefully so as not to blob any on the baseboards. She was actually having major doubts about the color, but since it had been her idea in the first place, she didn't feel she could back down on how terrific it was.

Faith was the least worried of the three. One year back home, she and her sister Sarah had painted their room bright red, and it had been kind of fun to be outrageous like that. So she just thought the whole thing was funny and said, "I'm just getting a little worried about the bats moving in."

"Well," Casey gave her estimation, "whatever it is or isn't, one thing for sure is that this is going to be the most talked about room on campus!"

"Oh my!" someone in the hallway behind Casey said. It was Alison Cavanaugh.

Alison did not fit at all the stereotypical image of housemother. She was only in her late twenties, and was very hip. Everything about her was a little larger than life. In the first place, she was big-boned. And then she had a huge mass of long, wavy brown hair that was always just this side of out-of-control. Her glasses were huge horn rims, which were always sliding down her nose. And most of her clothes were oversize sweaters and colorful caftan tops and loose-fitting pants of rough-weave cotton. Alison was big into natural fibers and natural foods.

It was hard to tell whether she was also big into black rooms. For the first few minutes, she just stood there and didn't say anything.

"Alison, come on, what do you think?" Dana prodded. Over the past year, Dana and Alison had become close friends in spite of the decade-plus difference in their ages. "Tell us it's the sharpest decorating idea you've ever seen."

"No. I went to the palace at Versailles, outside Paris, one summer, and the Hall of Mirrors there was sharper than this room."

"But you *do* like it?" Dana pushed a little more.

"I don't know if I'd go that far. Well, maybe. I guess I like it more than I would have thought, if you came up and told me you were going to paint your room black. Which, by the way, I don't seem to remember anyone doing." She gave them the fish eye, but they knew she wasn't really serious.

"Would you have let us do it if we *had* asked you beforehand?" Shelley asked.

"Probably not," Alison admitted.

"See," Shelley said, "we had to sneak."

"Now that it's nearly done, you're not going to make us paint it back, are you?" Faith moaned.

"No. I think you ought to suffer with it for a while. You know, I might even make a contribution. I have a black light and some day-glo posters from my brother's dorm room in the sixties."

"What's a black light?" Casey asked.

"Well, it looks like an ordinary fluorescent light, but if you hang it over day-glo posters, it makes the colors pop out all weird and luminescent."

"Great!" Dana said. "Everyone will think we're hippies."

"Everyone's probably going to think you're lunatics," Alison corrected. "Look. I only ask one thing. Keep your door shut, will you? Especially when you leave in the morning. Miss Allardyce doesn't come through the dorms very much, but every so often she makes a surprise check, and I've got a real strong feeling she would not be thrilled by this little decorating twist."

"But do we really have to worry about P.A.?" Shelley asked. "From what we saw the other night, it looks like she's got other things on her mind."

All the girls looked at Alison to catch her reaction to this, but there wasn't any. If she was curious about what they knew, she wasn't letting on. If she knew something herself, she wasn't telling. All she said was, "Well, I've got to take a box of Kleenex and a shoulder to cry on down to the second floor. I'm told there's a very homesick freshman there."

And with that, she was gone.

"Back in a minute," Dana said, and climbed down off her ladder and ran after Alison. She caught up with her near the broom closet, which was about the only private spot on the floor.

"Step into my office for a minute?" she asked Alison after she had managed to run around her and stop her in her tracks.

"Okay," Alison said.

When they got inside, Dana pressed.

"*Do* you know anything about Miss Allardyce and this gorgeous and *much* younger guy?"

Alison just shook her head.

"Does that mean no, you don't know? Or no, you're not telling?"

"It means there are things I can't tell even good friends like you. Please don't ask me again about this, Dana."

And off she went, leaving Dana standing between the vacuum cleaner and the wash bucket, feeling foolish.

CHAPTER FIVE

Shelley gave Tom a quick kiss on the front steps of Baker, breaking the most frequently broken rule at Canby Hall — No Kissing on Campus. He had surprised her by showing up outside her last class this afternoon, just to walk her back to the dorm.

This was the seventh time she had seen him in the week she had been back. Every time she turned around, he was there.

"I'm beginning to get the impression that you missed me this summer," she said.

"Oh Shel," he said. Tom was long on feelings, but didn't feel he had to put them into words. This was okay with Shelley. She had spent the past two months in Iowa with Paul, who talked all the time, about everything under the sun. It was one of the things she liked best about him. But it was nice now to be back with Tom, who she could just *be* with, without either of them having to say

36

a whole lot. She liked each guy for different reasons. Sometimes she thought it was a good thing she didn't live in one of those countries where girls her age got married. She felt light years away from being able to pick one guy and settle down with him forever.

"Where're you running off to now?" she asked Tom.

"Got to mow the lawn for my dad if he's going to give me the car tonight. Want to go for a ride?"

"I've got weeknight curfew. Ten o'clock. Plus I've got tons of homework. It'll have to be a short ride."

"I'll be by at seven. Look for a super-shiny Buick. After I finish the lawn, I'm supposed to wash the car. My dad drives a hard bargain."

Shelley trudged through the hot, stuffy stairwell, up the four flights to her room. She knew Faith would be over at the office of the *Canby Clarion*. She was now the school paper's chief photographer. And Dana would be at chorale practice. So Shelley expected to find 407 empty and ready for her to sneak in a quick nap before dinner. Back home, she used to take a nap every day after school. But here, there was usually so much going on, and so many girls hanging around 407 in the afternoon, and so much teasing from Dana and Faith about baby taking a nap and did she want her stuffed bunny and her teething ring, that she seldom did it anymore.

She pushed open the door to the room and was surprised to find Pamela Young sitting on her bed, reading a paperback. In her white shorts and white designer t-shirt, against the black wall with her spectacular California bronze tan, Pamela looked gorgeous. Everything about her was so dramatic. Shelley couldn't help being impressed.

Pamela looked up as if Shelley were the interloper, not her.

"Nice room," she said. It was hard for Shelley to tell if she was being sincere or sarcastic. Pamela's voice always had a slightly bored tone that made everything she said sound a little sarcastic. "I've been waiting for you quite a while."

"Oh," Shelley said, wishing she could come up with something a little more brilliant, but Pamela rattled her. Her ultracool manner made Shelley nervous.

"I'm dying of the heat," Pamela went on. "I'd like to go for a swim in that creek you mentioned, but I don't know how to get out there. I thought maybe you'd go over with me."

Shelley thought for a minute. Going would really mess up her plan to nap, then squeeze in an hour of French homework before dinner. But what the heck, it was too early in the term to worry about flunking out, and she suddenly wasn't that sleepy anymore. Then she thought about Faith. Was going with Pamela a betrayal of her roommate? She pushed the worry to the back of her mind.

"Okay," she said. "Just let me grab my suit." She was secretly flattered that out of all the girls on campus, Pamela had chosen her to go swimming with. Not that all the girls at Canby Hall would have wanted to go. After only a week, the campus population had pretty much split in two on the subject of Pamela Young.

Some of the girls thought she was incredibly sophisticated. She really *was* a friend of Michael Jackson. She actually *had* gone out on two or three dates with Matt Dillon. Stuck in the corner of her mirror was a snapshot of her and Jennifer Beal from "Flashdance." The two of them were at the beach — leaning against opposite sides of a stood-up surfboard.

Unfortunately, though, everyone who Shelley respected fell into the camp that thought Pamela was a snob and a bigmouthed braggart.

"If she were really cool," Casey had said, "she would never mention all the famous people she knows."

"Plus," Dana had added, "who she knows doesn't say anything about her. Her mother's a big star. So the people she hangs out with are other big stars. My mom's a fashion buyer. So I get a lot of free clothes samples. So I get to be better dressed than a lot of girls. But I don't think it makes me any better than anyone else. My mom brings home clothes. Pamela's mother brings home movie stars. Big deal. That stuff doesn't say anything about *us*. Just about where we were lucky enough to arrive on this planet. Plus, my guess is that most of those big stars think she's as big a drip as we think she is."

"Not me," Faith had said dryly. "I'm just crazy about that girl."

So Shelley knew that if anyone spotted her out at the creek this afternoon with Pamela, she would take a lot of flak. But it seemed worth the risk. The glamour that surrounded Pamela was just too irresistible.

"I heard you were a big swimmer around here," Pamela said when they were walking out the road toward the creek, bathing suits on under their shorts and t-shirts, towels thrown over their shoulders.

"Naw," Shelley said modestly. "I dropped off the team when drama club started taking all my time. Now I only swim a couple of times a week, just workouts for myself."

"Our pool isn't really big enough for laps. I'm trying to get Yvonne to put in an Olympic-size. Now what we mostly do is work out with Jane Fonda."

"Oh yes, me too," Shelley said. "I have the book."

"Not the book, dope, I mean Yvonne and I go over to Jane's and work out with *her*."

"Oh," Shelley said. *Oh* was all she could find to say in response to a lot of the things Pamela said.

Since it was late in the afternoon, and a

weekday, the creek wasn't as crowded as it might have been. Still, there *were* a few kids Shelley knew, and she could see them bend their heads to whisper to each other after they had said hi to Shelley and noted who she was hanging out with.

Everything about Pamela was noticed. Mostly because she was so noticeable. Nothing about her was usual or ordinary. Nothing about her fit in easily with Canby Hall. Shelley figured that part of this was coming from California and not knowing how things were done here, how girls dressed, how they talked. But she was beginning to see that a bigger part of it was that Pamela *liked* being different, and worked at keeping it that way.

For instance, everyone else out at the creek had brought a towel. Most were plain bath towels. Some were a little rattier than others, with unraveled edges. Some were colored, some white, some had flower print patterns, but basically they were towels taken out of family linen closets. A few kids had actual beach towels with pictures printed on them, but nothing remarkable. And then there was Pamela. She opened her towel and spread it out on the sloping bank. Stenciled on the white background in green printing were the words *Paramount Pictures — Mr. Gere*. It was clearly a studio towel provided for Richard Gere on the set of one of his pictures.

Then there was her swimsuit, which was of some amazing shiny, space-age fabric in brilliant purple. And, of course, Pamela had a perfect body.

All those mornings working out with Jane, Shelley thought.

Once Pamela had staked out her turf, she looked around. "So this is your little creek," she said.

"Well, *we* like it," Shelley said defensively. The creek was one of her favorite spots around Greenleaf.

"Yes, I'm sure you do. But you have to understand, I have friends back home with *bathtubs* bigger than this. I mean, sweetheart, Malibu it ain't."

Pamela eyed the water. "I don't suppose it's heated," she said.

Shelley laughed. "It takes your breath away at first. You really should get into it sort of gradually."

But Shelley knew the advice would go unheeded. Easing into the water would be too boring for Pamela. She had to run full-tilt down the slope, take a flying leap off the bank, do a racing dive that creased the surface of the water, and come out of it with a squeal that got the attention of the few kids left who weren't already watching her.

Shelley followed Pamela into the water and swam over to her with a few strong strokes.

"I think I'm losing all feeling in my toes," Pamela said. "I'd better get out."

"Come on," Shelley said, "I'll show you the rope swing."

Pamela reluctantly followed Shelley up

onto the bank where one end of the rope was tied around the trunk of a tree. The other end was high up, tied to a branch that hung out over the creek. Shelley freed the rope so it was ready to go.

"What's this?" Pamela asked, but her voice was totally void of interest. "Some quaint little summer sport?"

"Well," Shelley said, sorry she had started this, but not knowing how to get out of it now, "the idea is to get a running start from back up here" — Shelley demonstrated — "then run and hang on as the rope swings across. Then you wait until you swing back out over the middle of the creek and then let go. Here, I'll show you."

When she climbed out, she handed the rope to Pamela.

"You want to try it?"

"Not really," Pamela said, then looked around. Three guys on a blanket on the opposite bank were watching her. Seeing she had an audience, Pamela changed her mind. "Oh, all right. Give it to me."

Pamela took one turn on the rope swing, then came out with the comment, "Charming."

"You know," Shelley told her, "It's good form to get the rope back up here when you're done. That way the next person can use it without having to go in and fetch it."

Pamela received this piece of information without much interest. "Well, I suppose they'll live if they have to go in this once, won't they now?"

Shelley took a fast dive and brought the rope up herself. When she rejoined Pamela on the towels, they sat around and dried off while Pamela told Shelley the kinds of things she did for fun in California. It sounded like she went to more parties in a week than Shelley went to in a year. And they weren't just Cokes and chips and playing records and dancing parties, like the ones Shelley was used to.

"Once I got this invitation — you know, very formal, calligraphy on cream stationery — saying the party would begin at Los Angeles International Airport on Saturday night at seven. This was Greg's bash and his folks are so rich they make Yvonne look like a pauper, and so everyone knew something really wild was up."

"So what happened?" Shelley asked, trying not to appear too interested.

"Well, we all got to the airport and there was a private jet waiting. There was dinner on board and party games, but Greg wouldn't tell any of us where the plane was headed. When we got off, we were in Hawaii."

"What did your parents say? How did you get off school? I mean, you didn't fly back that night?" Shelley couldn't imagine something like this happening back in Pine Bluff. Or at Canby Hall.

"We stayed three days. His parents had called ours beforehand. It was only the kids

who were in the dark this time. For a change."
Pamela gave a snide little laugh here. "And
as for school, well nobody out there thinks
it's very important. Not like these dopes here.
They really think all this academic stuff
matters. Which reminds me, do you know
some brain around here who needs some
extra cash and wants to do my papers for
me? I pay quite well."

"Do your papers?" Shelley was really surprised now.

"Yes, of course," Pamela said. "So I can
pass these stupid courses, and keep Yvonne
happy, and still have time for the important
things in life. Like having dinner at the
Auberge. Have you been there? It's where I've
been eating mostly. Not bad for a French restaurant in the middle of Nowhere Junction."

She went on.

"And I need at least two hours a day if I'm
going to keep up my tennis game. And I need
whole free days to slip off to New York to
shop. A lifestyle like mine requires time to
maintain it, sweetheart. Plus I may have even
more of my precious hours taken up by a
certain someone. I can't believe I've managed
to find someone moderately interesting out
here in the wilderness."

"Who?" Shelley was curious as to who
Pamela Young would find interesting after
hanging out with guys who had parties on
planes.

"His name's Bret Harper. Know him?"

"Oh, Pamela. Don't. Dana went with him

all last year and got hurt bad. He's Mister Love 'Em and Leave 'Em."

"But you're talking about loving and leaving typical Canby Hall girls, aren't you — girls like Dana?"

"Dana's sharp as they come, Pamela." Shelley came to her roommate's defense.

"Oh yes, I forgot," Pamela said. "She lives in *New York*, doesn't she? Such a little sophisticate. I hear she's even been to the ballet. I should call Rudi and have him come up for lunch one day. We could ask Dana to come along. Do you think she'd enjoy a little lobster salad and some shop talk with Nureyev?"

Pamela paused and looked at Shelley. She didn't usually. Usually she looked off into space as she talked, as if she were a great actress onstage, giving a big speech.

"You know, Michelle" — she was the first person to call Shelley that practically since her birth — "you're really the only girl I've met here who has any *real* sophistication."

Shelley couldn't help beaming under this soft spotlight of attention. Pamela cut into it with the rest of her thought on the matter.

"Which is really incredible considering you come from Hogwash Hollow, or wherever."

CHAPTER SIX

Dana was dancing at a grand ball in Vienna. Everyone was wearing old-fashioned long formal gowns with whirling skirts. She must be back in the nineteenth century. But then why was *she* wearing her grubbiest jeans — the ones with a rip at the knee — and a Linda Ronstadt t-shirt? How embarrassing.

And who was she dancing with? Randy? In a full-dress uniform with a chestful of medals? What was going on here?

Gradually, Dana opened her eyes and realized this was a dream, triggered by the "Blue Danube Waltz" pinging out of her digital watch. She vaguely remembered setting the alarm and putting it under her pillow.

But why did she want to get up in the middle of the night? She sat up and looked around. Through the tiny cracks in the venetian blinds at the windows, she could see a bluish light outside. So it wasn't the middle of the night after all. She and Faith and Dana were finding that the black paint job made it seem like night a lot of the time in 407.

She pulled the watch out and pushed off the alarm and looked at the time. Six a.m. Now what could she have wanted to do that would require getting out of bed at this absurd hour? She burrowed her head back into the pillow and tried to remember.

Class? No — no classes started that early. Besides, it was Saturday.

Saturday. That was a clue. Something she was going to do on a Saturday morning.

See the dawn with Randy! That was it! He was supposed to come by in his pick-up at quarter to seven and drive her out to an overlook he loved, and show her a Massachusetts sunrise. The only other one she'd seen was last spring. But that one had been outside her window, and had gone hardly noticed as she came into the homestretch of ten straight hours of coffee-fueled cramming for her history exam.

This was a different kind of dawn-watching entirely. It was just the kind of close-to-nature sort of thing that Randy did all the time . . . and wanted her to do with him. Last Sunday night, he had rushed over and breathlessly gotten her out of Baker to run over to his family's stable so she could see a foal being born. Coming from New York City, she had never seen anything like this before. He really was opening up a whole new world to her.

Once she remembered why she was supposed to get up, she bolted out of bed, and ran down to the fourth floor washroom. Not surprisingly, she had the place to herself. She took a shower in the big, blue-tiled stall. She loved the smell of this place — the scents of hundreds of bars of soap used by nearly a century of Canby Hall girls.

When she got out, she combed her long brown hair in front of the mirror and started blowing it dry, bending from the waist and brushing it up from underneath. Her hair was so thick that it usually took her forever to get it dry. This morning, though, after she had been drying for maybe five minutes, the power suddenly went out. Dana stood up and found an extremely annoyed and bleary-eyed Ellie Bolton glowering at her. She was holding the just-pulled plug to Dana's dryer in her hand.

"Morrison," she said. "It's barely past the crack of dawn on one of the two mornings a week that I don't have to get woken up by the blow dryers of thirty girls."

Unlucky Ellie lived in 415, the room directly across from the washroom. She was always putting up notes on the long mirror, asking the rest of the girls to please not talk so loudly while they were in there. Or run the water too hard.

"Sorry, Ellie," Dana said. "Great morning, though, isn't it?"

"I don't know," Ellie said, yawning and starting back to her room. "I'm hoping I don't find out. My plan is to miss it entirely."

Well, she'd have to meet the dawn with damp hair, Dana thought. She looked at herself long and hard in the mirror. She didn't usually do this. Usually someone else was around and if you started gaping at yourself, you almost surely were going to get teased around Canby Hall. Especially a girl like Dana, who everyone thought was probably vain because she was so pretty.

The secret, though, was that although Dana knew that she was considered one of the best-looking girls around Canby Hall, she herself didn't think she was all that great. She thought her nose was too long and her lips too full and that when she smiled, instead of looking happy, she looked like a goony lunatic. She tried it now in front of the mirror, smiling as if Randy were coming up the walk in front of Baker and she was just about to say hi to him. She froze the smile on her face and tried to judge it objectively.

Yep, she thought. *I look like a goony lunatic.*

Now Cheryl Stein, *she* was good-looking, Dana thought, then wondered if Cheryl secretly thought her hair was too lusciously auburn, her teeth too pearly white, her eyes too deeply blue? Maybe the secret was that every girl at Canby Hall went around think-

ing they weren't as good-looking as they really
were.

Dana caught herself. *Earth to Dana,* she
thought. *Better step on it, or you won't see
this sunrise until noon.*

She dashed back to the room and changed
quickly, pulling on the same old jeans she'd
been wearing at the Viennese ball. She rum-
maged through her drawers, but couldn't find
the Linda Ronstadt t-shirt. She settled for a
plum-colored polo shirt.

Randy was waiting when she got downstairs, sitting in the cab of his beat-up old
pick-up truck, reading a book.

"What're you reading?" she asked him.

"It's this guy who writes all about his life
as a veterinarian."

Randy read a lot, on his own. He was
seventeen and had graduated from Greenleaf
High last June. Now he worked on his family's
land. They had a big horse ranch, and an
apple orchard. This was what he wanted to
do with his life. He didn't want to go to college. "The outdoors is my major," he had told
her once.

Dana wasn't sure what she thought about
this. She respected his sureness, but thought
he might be limiting himself by not at least
trying college. She wanted to talk with him
about this, but it still seemed too soon.

"Lend it to me when you're finished?" she
asked now, tapping the book with her fore-
finger.

"Sure," he said, and started up the truck with a roar. They barreled down the driveway, and headed toward the low, rolling hills just beyond Greenleaf.

"Where's this mystery spot you're taking me to?" Dana shouted over the noise of the engine and the jostling truck body, and the radio, which he always had turned up and tuned in to the local country station.

Dana often embarrassed herself in front of Randy by bursting into tears at one or another of these songs. Some of them were just too sad for her to bear. There was one called *Down to My Last Broken Heart* that was so tear-making she had to shut off the radio as soon as she heard it coming on, or risk crying for a straight fifteen minutes.

"Up in the hills" was all Randy would say. "I want to surprise you. I've never taken anybody up there before."

Dana felt a little thrill when Randy talked to her like this. But she still didn't think this was going to be a major romance. They were just so different. Besides, she had let herself fall head over heels for Bret Harper last year, and where had that gotten her? Shot down. She wasn't going to make that mistake again.

The morning was beginning to come on strong — the hills in the middle distance were beginning to be covered with a creamy blue sky. The sun peeking above the tops of the hills was yawning and gathering force for the day ahead.

"It's almost about to happen," Randy said. "We should make it just in time."

Soon he veered off the highway onto a gravel-covered dirt road that switched back and forth along the side of the highest hill. Further along, he veered off that onto a steeply inclined road that was really two parallel ruts gouged out of the earth by the wheels of previous visitors.

"Is this a popular place?" Dana asked.

"Well, I think it used to be. It's called Lovers' Leap. I guess couples with big problems — you know, her family wouldn't let her marry him, or vice versa, or one of them was already promised to someone else, that kind of stuff — used to come here. Well, I think the history is that they used to throw themselves off the edge here."

"Really!?" Dana gasped.

"Oh, I don't know. Could be someone just gave it the name to add a little glamour. At any rate, I've never seen anyone jump. Actually, in all the time I've been coming up here — usually to think about important stuff — I've never seen another living soul."

"Pretty early in the morning to be bringing me up to such a romantic place," Dana teased.

"We country boys know it's the early bird that catches the worm."

Dana punched him in the arm, smiling. "Worm! Thanks!"

He put an arm around her shoulder and pulled her closer to him.

"Just around this bend's as far as we can

go in the truck," he said. "We have to take the last part on foot. There's just a narrow path."

When they came through the trees around the curve into the clearing, Randy let out a long, low whistle.

"This is really weird," he said. "I've been coming here for years and I've never seen any other cars. And today, and at this hour, there are two!"

"Yeah," Dana said, distractedly. Her thoughts were racing. One of the cars was a rusted-out beater, an old black Camaro. The one beside it, though, was unmistakable. Even without its "CH 1" plates, she'd know that burgundy Buick with the custom navy interior anywhere — it was Patrice Allardyce's car!

"Randy!" Dana whispered excitedly.

"Why are you whispering?" he whispered back, teasing. "There's nobody around but us."

"That's our headmistress' car!"

He looked puzzled. "What would she be doing out here?" he asked.

"That's what I'd like to know," Dana said. Then, after thinking for a few seconds, said, "Or maybe I wouldn't like to know. Let's get out of here. I think something might be going on that's too personal. I'm curious, but I don't want to embarrass anyone."

"I think," Randy said, looking over Dana's shoulder, out the open window of the truck's cab, "I think we might be just a little too late for that."

Dana turned around to see what he was looking at. It was Patrice Allardyce all right, not in her usual silks and tweeds, but in old khakis and a striped button-down shirt with the tails out, and dusty tennis shoes on her feet. She was running out of the woods towards her car.

Following her were shouts — "Please stop!"

And following the shouts was the person shouting them, the same young blond guy who'd been with the headmistress in her living room that night. Today he was wearing black jeans and a black shirt and his long hair was rumpled, as if he hadn't combed it yet.

Patrice Allardyce looked a little rumpled herself. Her hair, usually pulled up and back in a beauty-shoppy way, was hanging loose around her shoulders now, tousled by the wind as she ran. She had no makeup on either. This, as far as Dana could remember, was a first. Usually, Patrice looked as though she had put on her lipstick in the morning, and then been careful not to touch anything to her lips all day, to keep it perfectly set.

Dana didn't have time for any more amazed gawking at the headmistress because, within seconds of bursting out of the woods, she saw Dana sitting in the truck, and froze. She looked like a panicked rabbit in the headlights of an oncoming car.

The young guy, being further behind, at first didn't see anything, just kept coming, shouting for her to stop. Once he saw her frozen to the ground, though, he looked up into the stares of Randy and Dana. By this time, he was right behind P.A. He put his hands on her shoulders, as if to protect her.

And then suddenly, the old Patrice Allardyce was back. She took a deep breath, inhaling all the dignity she could muster, squared her shoulders, and with one hand pulled her hair back.

"Good morning, Dana," she said and nodded, as if they were just passing each other on a campus path.

"Good morning Ms. Allardyce," Dana said.

"A little early to be out on a date, isn't it?" she said, giving Dana her best headmistress glower.

"We're just going up to see the sunrise," Dana said, trying frantically to remember if there was a Canby Hall rule against watching suns rise.

"All right then. You'd better get going, I suppose, or you'll miss it entirely."

Dana looked at Randy with a big question mark in her eyes. He picked up on her confusion and took charge of the situation. He climbed out of the cab, came around, and opened her door.

"This way, Dana," he said, guiding her smoothly past Patrice Allardyce and the mystery man, who had taken his hands off P.A.'s shoulders and was just standing behind her, breathing heavily from having run so hard after her.

* * *

When Dana and Randy got far enough into the woods to be sure they wouldn't be heard, he asked her, "What was *that* little scene about?"

"Search me," Dana said. "Nobody knows much of anything about Patrice Allardyce. It's as if she only exists as headmistress of Canby Hall, as if there's no private person behind the public one. I guess I never believed that. I knew she had to have some personal life. But, I'll tell you, whatever I thought, it wasn't this. This guy must be ten years younger than her."

"At least," Randy said. "And he's not from around these parts. I know all the locals."

"And he's so . . ." Dana reached for the word she wanted. "So *wild*-looking. I mean if I were going to match P.A. up with someone in my mind, it would be someone like Alistair Cooke on "Masterpiece Theater" — someone real elegant and older. Someone who would take P.A. out to the symphony, or to an art gallery. This guy, in addition to being so young, looks like he hangs out at dragstrips, and bars where there are about three fights every night."

"I don't know," Randy said, taking Dana's hand and leading her further up the path. "They say opposites attract."

"But not *that* opposite!" Dana said.

"Hey, here we are," Randy said. "Lovers' Leap." They were now at the top of the hill. Below them were the rolling grazing lands

and patchwork plots of farms that surrounded Greenleaf.

"Oh," Dana said and sighed. "It's beautiful,
Randy. You're showing me so much." She
paused a moment, her face pulling into a
look of worry.

"What is it, Dana?" Randy sounded
concerned.

"Lovers' Leap. Oh Randy. You don't think
they came up here to leap, do you?"

CHAPTER SEVEN

Dana was sitting in her ancient history class. Mrs. Flood was standing in front of her roll-down map of ancient Europe and Asia. The map had seen many years of jabbing from Mrs. Flood's pointer, and was by now pretty bedraggled. She was lecturing on the Phoenicians today, and had the rubber tip of the pointer gouged into Phoenicia.

Mrs. Flood always had her pointer in hand. When she wasn't using it to point out countries, she was using it to call on students. Once Dana ran into her at a Friday night mixer dance that Mrs. Flood was chaperoning, and almost didn't recognize her. She realized later that it was because she didn't have her pointer with her.

Usually Dana loved this class. Mrs. Flood was a dramatic lecturer. Her classes were never boring. When she really got going, it was like watching one of those big old Technicolor epic movies about ancient Rome or Greece or Egypt.

But today, Dana kept drifting off from what Mrs. Flood was saying. She kept sliding from the Phoenicians to Patrice Allardyce. She couldn't stop wondering what was going on with her and The Guy. (Dana didn't know his name, and so had come to think of him as just The Guy.)

She had told Shelley and Faith about running into them at Lovers' Leap. Each had her own opinion on the matter.

"She's got this secret passion," Shelley said matter-of-factly, as if she had just read it in *People* magazine. "Something very different from the image she puts out around here. Maybe it *is* drag racing. Something like that. Maybe she shoots pool. Anyway, that's where she met this guy. And she fell in love with him. And he fell in love with her. But she couldn't tell him who she was. She couldn't let him into this side of her life. But he found out anyway and now here he is, and she's going to have to decide between continuing here as headmistress of Canby Hall, or running off with him and working as part of his pit crew at the dragstrip."

Faith and Dana exploded with laughter at this fantasy. Shelley was miffed.

"You just wait and see," she said smugly.

"There's a simple explanation somewhere," Faith, always the practical one, said. "My guess is that he's a juvenile delinquent who she's taken under her wing. You know — one

of those programs where they show tough
kids a bunch of nature stuff and it gets them
to give up their life of crime."

"You haven't seen this guy up close," Dana
protested. "He's a lot younger than P.A., but
he's too old to be a juvenile delinquent. He's
at least twenty-five."

As she was walking back to Baker after
history class, still thinking about the mystery
of Ms. Allardyce and The Guy, coming out
of the administration building on a path that
was going to run straight across hers was
Patrice Allardyce! It was almost as though
Dana's thinking about her had conjured her
up.

Dana grew nervous, although rationally,
she wasn't the one who had something to be
nervous about. Still, she would rather not
have to run into the headmistress again so
soon. She didn't know if she should say something about the morning they'd met, or just
pretend it hadn't happened. Even though it
had provided her with an incredibly juicy
tidbit of gossip, Dana was beginning to wish
she had never seen Patrice Allardyce up at
Lovers' Leap.

And she was really wishing that the headmistress was not, at this very moment, about
ten feet away and headed straight for her.
Unless Dana suddenly developed the ability
to lift off the ground like a helicopter, she
was going to have to say hello.

"Hello, Ms. Allardyce," she said and nodded,

hoping this would be enough and she could just keep walking.

"Hello, Dana," Patrice Allardyce said and stopped. "Did you have a nice sunrise to watch?"

"Oh, yes, thank you," Dana said in her super-polite, speaking-to-authority voice.

"I'm always happy when my girls take an interest in nature. I myself am such a lover of nature. I do a lot of hiking, you know."

"No, I didn't," Dana said.

"And a lot of bird-watching. I was up there Saturday morning with one of the members of my bird-watching club. We were quite excited at having sighted and identified a rare type of bullfinch."

"Oh, that's nice," Dana said. She waited until she was about twenty feet down the path, away from the headmistress before she expressed her true sentiments.

"Who do you think you're kidding?" she said.

CHAPTER EIGHT

It looked like a funeral. Dana, Faith, and Shelley sat in the blackness of 407, all dressed up, in total silence.

The occasion for the dressing up, the silence, and the waiting was the same — Pamela Young was taking them all out to dinner at the Auberge, the French restaurant where Pamela had been eating most nights as a way of avoiding the Canby Hall dining room.

Faith and Dana were as excited as if they were about to go off and plunge a stopped drain. Faith was still holding onto the memory of Pamela treating her as if she were the hired help. Dana, in the course of a few conversations when Pamela was around with Shelley, had formed the opinion that Pamela was "a nerd in sheep's clothing." She thought Pamela dressed great, but was a loser in every other way.

"Shel," Dana had said, "the girl's got one

topic of conversation — herself. She never seems to get tired of it, but *I* do."

Dana and Faith were only going out to dinner with Pamela under pressure from Shelley, who wanted them to give Pamela one more chance.

"A lot of her showing off is just to cover her insecurity about being new here," Shelley told them, even though she secretly suspected Pamela wasn't insecure at all, just a show-off.

"And she didn't mean to offend Faith. She's real sorry now, but she's too shy to apologize." This one was a total lie. When Shelley had informed Pamela that Faith was still angry, Pamela's response had been, "Too bad."

But then Pamela *had* offered to treat them all to this dinner.

"Yvonne'll pick up the tab," she told Shelley. "And then I can get her off my back by telling her that I *am* making some friends around here."

Shelley was counting on Pamela being full of great stories about her star-studded life in California tonight. Then Faith and Dana would see how neat it was hanging out with someone so totally glamourous. Shelley still had the fantasy that Pamela would take them all home at Thanksgiving. That Yvonne would send a Lear jet to pick them up. That Pamela would fix them all up with dates. Michael Jackson for Faith. Matt Dillon for Dana. Timothy Hutton for Shelley. It was a pretty well-developed fantasy by now.

* * *

Pamela had told them she would be by with a taxi around quarter to six. It was now nearly six-thirty. Faith looked at her watch and sighed.

"I'm about ready to throw in the towel and go down to the cafeteria, even though I hear tonight it's cod patties."

"I know," Dana agreed. "I'm about to starve. Maybe I'll open a can of Spaghetti-Os, just to take the edge off."

"Dana," Shelley said, shaking her head, "you must have a hundred-mile-per-hour metabolism. You eat all the time and still stay skinny as a rail. Only *you* could consider a can of Spaghetti-Os a snack. But don't. I hear the food's terrific at the Auberge and I know Pamela's going to be here any minute now."

On this cheery promise, the three of them fell into fifteen more minutes of gloomy silence, before there was the honking of a taxi from the driveway below.

"Now that it's finally time to go," Faith said, "I suddenly *really* don't want to. Pamela Young is just bound to do or say something to give me indigestion. She won't be able to help herself."

"Faith," Shelley pleaded. "She's better than you think. All I want you two to do is give her this one more chance. I mean, how much of a hardship am I asking you to go through — sitting for a couple of hours getting a free French dinner? I mean do you really think you can bear up? And if you still don't like her after tonight, I'll never ask you to have anything more to do with her. I promise."

Pamela was waiting for them in the cab. In the same show-offy way that she over-dressed for classes and on-campus activities, she was now show-offily *under* dressed for going to a French restaurant. All she was wearing was a Hawaiian print shirt, jeans, and sandals, in contrast to the three room-mates, who were wearing their best summer outfits. Dana had on a cotton dress in a tomato red color. Faith was wearing a white linen skirt and a blue silk shirt. Shelley had on a raw silk skirt and a striped shirt that picked up the green of the skirt — her most dynamite outfit.

Pamela didn't bother to make apologies for being late, just launched into telling them what she'd been doing.

"I was on long distance with Yvonne," she said as they started off in the taxi. "She's going out with Burt Reynolds tonight. I told her she must be the last woman in Hollywood to date him. She was also the last woman in Hollywood to date Warren Beatty. Still, it's better that she just sticks to dating. At least she hasn't been getting married lately. That's where the real disaster comes in — for her *and* for me. You should see some of the gobblers I've had to call Daddy. It's gotten so I think marriage is the stupid part and divorce is the sensible solution."

"I don't know about that," Dana disagreed.

"Dana's folks got divorced last year," Shelley explained to Pamela. "She misses her dad."

"Oh," Pamela said, patting Dana's shoulder. "you'll lighten up about that when you see how profitable the situation can be. You can really guilt-trip both of them about getting divorced. And then you can play them off against each other. You can double your allowance. And wait until Christmas. Believe me, you play it right and that divorce could be the best thing that ever happened to you."

"She's not hardhearted enough to think like that," Faith said, speaking up for Dana, who was now looking out the open window, saying nothing.

A thick silence fell over the four of them like a low-lying cloud. Pamela acted as if she didn't notice the tension, or didn't care about it. She pulled out her cigarettes and lit one up. Faith immediately began coughing.

"She's bothered by smoke since she was sick last summer," Dana explained to Pamela, who at first didn't respond at all to this information. Dana just kept staring, and finally, without saying anything, Pamela crushed the cigarette out in the ashtray.

"Fun bunch," she muttered under her breath, pulling out her nail file and going into a major manicure, sprinkling white powdery filings all over Shelley's skirt. Shelley noticed, but didn't particularly care. She was too busy worrying about how terribly this was going so far, and trying to figure out what she could do to turn things around, to make her roommates see what fun Pamela could be if you gave her a chance.

Luckily, the Auberge wasn't far, and so they didn't have to ride for long in the horrible, awkward silence.

It was a pretty place — an old country cottage with blue shutters and vines practically covering it. It had been converted into a restaurant a few years back, a pretty expensive one. None of the roommates had ever been there. Mostly they ate in the dining hall since it was already paid for. Sometimes they went on dates at Pizza Pete's. Sometimes they went to the Big Burger, but that was about as fancy as they got. Dana had been to a few good restaurants in New York, but the other two had never been anywhere like this. When they walked through the door and saw all the brocade and candlelight and plush beige carpeting, they shifted their focus from hating Pamela to trying to live up to the atmosphere and appear sophisticated.

Almost immediately, a small man in a tuxedo came up to greet them. Pamela, who had been acting like she owned the place, was now acting as if this guy were an extremely old and dear friend. She held out her hand for him to bend and kiss, which he did.

"Ooooo Georges," she cooed, "*Vous êtes vraiment de trop.*"

"She's telling him he's simply too much,"

Faith translated for Dana. Faith had had one year of French, Dana none.

"She's not!" Dana whispered. "Of course, I don't know why anything she says surprises me anymore."

Pamela was still busy trading French pleasantries with Georges, and so didn't hear this exchange. Now, though, she looked at Dana and Faith and Shelley as though she had just remembered they were with her.

"*Vous avez une bonne table pour moi et mes amies?*" she asked Georges.

"She's asking for a good table," Faith translated again. "As opposed to one where the wood is rotting, I guess."

This time Pamela heard and shot Faith a look that could kill.

"I've been bilingual all my life, Faith. I guess I forget that some people haven't. I'll try to remember to gear things down to everyone's level."

Georges showed them to a big round table in the corner of the restaurant. It was covered in white linen, with a silver vase of roses in the center. The napkins were puffed up like pocket handkerchiefs and stuck in the large, leaded crystal water goblets.

"It's not much, I know," Pamela said when they had all sat down, "but they've got a pretty nice little *coq au vin* and some not bad *saumon fumé.* Oh, Dana, that's chicken in wine sauce and smoked salmon."

This time it was Dana who shot The Look That Could Kill. She opened her menu and said, "Do they have hamburgers here?"

Shelley was desperate. She tried to think of some way to put things on track, to show off Pamela to better advantage. The best path seemed to be to get her to talk about her life in California.

"Pamela, is your mother still exercising with Jane Fonda?"

"Oh no," Pamela said, "she has to be in on the very latest. The in thing now is this guy who comes around in a truck. He's got a complete gym inside and gives you a workout in your own driveway. Sometimes she has friends over to work out with her. Victoria Principal. Ryan and Farrah. Paul and Joanne."

"You mean Paul Newman and Joanne Woodward?!" Shelley said. "Boy!"

Dana and Faith sat silent. Faith took a piece of French bread off a little silver serving dish. She buttered it and ate it and when she was finished, turned to Pamela and said, "My mom jogs on Saturday mornings with Clara Robinson and Eileen Stevens."

"Who are they?" Pamela said.

"Friends of hers. Clara runs a yarn shop in Georgetown. Eileen's a medical technician."

"How interesting," Pamela said sarcastically.

"About as interesting as who your mother pumps iron with. Usually we talk about ourselves and *our* lives — not who our parents hang out with."

Pamela looked like a rhino who has just been given a shot by zoo people trying to capture her — one of those injections that doesn't kill the animal, just stuns it in its tracks. She didn't say anything, just began to cry. The three girls sat and watched in astonishment as the tears rolled down Pamela's cheeks.

"Oh, hey, Pam," Faith said, "I didn't mean to go that far. Really. I even take it back. You want to talk about your mom, it's cool with me."

"Me, too," Dana rushed in. "I love her movies. I'm really a big fan."

Pamela didn't say anything, just continued to sit there sniffling and looking horribly hurt and dabbing at her eyes with the corner of her linen napkin.

The others felt awful — Shelley because she really liked Pamela, Faith and Dana because, even though they didn't like her much, neither did they want to make *anyone* this obviously miserable.

After a few minutes of everyone just sitting there, no one knowing quite how to save the situation, there was suddenly a new presence hovering above them. They all felt it at about the same time and looked up.

It was Bret Harper, Dana's old flame and Pamela's new one. He was all dressed up in a khaki suit and white shirt and navy tie.

"Hi," he said to the table in general, but really to Pamela in particular. "This is really funny running into you. My parents are up from Boston, taking me out to dinner. I just spotted you from across the room." Apparently from that distance he hadn't noticed the deep gloom that the four of them were sunk into.

The three roommates looked down at their plates. Dana hated running into Bret under the best of circumstances, and especially hated him coming over mainly to see Pamela. Faith and Shelley were just embarrassed by the whole situation — Bret and Dana and old wounds and Pamela crying, the whole mess. But then suddenly the mess disappeared.

"Oooooo Bret!" Pamela was saying, cooing in the same ooozy voice she had used on Georges, the maitre d'. "I can't believe you're here! And I've never seen you in a suit before!"

The other three looked up at her in amazement. The tears of a minute ago were completely gone. Her expression was as bright and sparkly as if she were about to blow out the candles on her birthday cake, or as if she had just gotten an all-A report card. The tears had apparently been an act, completely phony.

Bret only stayed a couple of minutes before excusing himself. "Got to get back to the folks. Nice seeing you, girls. I'll call you tonight, Pam, when I get back to the dorm."

"Well, well," Pamela said when he was

gone, "you never know who you're going to run into when you eat out." She was looking at Dana as she said this, gloating over having hooked the one who got away from Dana. Then she opened the large menu that was on the plate in front of her.

"Oh my, am I hungry," she said. "What do you say we start off with some of the paté? It's a little peasantish, but tasty."

Dana pushed her chair back and got up before saying, "Thanks anyway, Pamela, but I think I'm going back to Baker for some of the peasantish cod patties. I guess for me, the company's more important than the food."

Faith was the next to get up. "Guess I'll go with her," she said. "Thanks anyway, Pam. And you'll have to show me sometime that little trick you do with tears. I guess when your mother's an actress, you can pick up a lot of stuff like that."

Shelley didn't know what to do. Her roommates had left. She could follow them. It was true that Pamela had behaved awfully. But still, it seemed too cruel to leave her all alone at the table, especially with Bret across the room to see it. And so she picked up her menu and looked over the list of appetizers.

"You're not going with them?" Pamela sounded truly surprised.

"No, I'll stay," Shelley said. "But instead of the paté, can I have a shrimp cocktail?"

When Shelley got back to 407 later that night, Faith and Dana were studying at their desks. They looked up as she came into the room.

"How was dinner?" Dana asked, but her voice was filled with bitterness, not curiosity.

"I'm sorry, Dana," Shelley said. "I know you're not happy about her and Bret, but really — it's a free country. He's not your boyfriend anymore, so really — why shouldn't she date him?"

"It's not her dating him that I mind. It's her giving me that sickening look, as though she was taking him away from me. One thing Pamela's not short on is ego."

"She's better, you know," Shelley said, "when she's just with me, alone."

"Then that's how you ought to keep it," Faith said. "Personally, I'd like to be counted out of any more nights like this one."

"Ditto," Dana said. "I think you've got a right to pick your own friends, Shel, but I think you ought to just give up on getting us all to be big buddies. It's just not going to happen."

"I know, I know," Shelley said, admitting defeat. "I just had this terrific fantasy about us all going out there with her and getting fixed up with all these hunky movie stars."

"Oh Shel," Dana moaned. "I'd rather go out with Ricky Purcell, with his acne and greasy glasses and a whole night of his talk about cars than get fixed up with Matt Dillon, if it was Pamela doing the fixing."

Shelley fell silent for a while, then looked

at Faith and Dana and said, "She's not as bad as you think."

"I think she is," Faith said. "Actually, I think she might even be worse than we think. And I think sooner or later you're going to discover that for yourself. And when you do. . . ."

"I know, don't come running to you," Shelley said.

"No," Faith said, breaking into a slow smile, "that's when you should definitely come running to us. That's when you'll really need us."

CHAPTER NINE

Casey Flint sat on the just-mowed lawn in front of the Canby Hall chapel. She pulled from the pocket of her khakis a folded note, opened it and reread it.

Casey,
Please meet me at four when I get out of chorale practice. I need to talk to you in private.

Dana

She couldn't think what Dana could be wanting to talk with her about alone. What couldn't she say in front of Shelley and Faith? Was she having some trouble with them?

She didn't have long to mull over any of these speculations before the heavy oak doors of the chapel opened and the twenty or so members of the Canby Hall chorale came spilling out onto the front steps. Dana was talking with a couple of them, but made a quick good-bye when she saw Casey, and came running over.

"Got time to go for a walk with me?" Dana asked, reaching down to give Casey a hand, then pulling her to her feet.

"Sure. My curiosity's killing me. I'm dying to know what warrants all this meeting-like-spies stuff."

"Well, you've got the right word," Dana said. "It's spying I want to talk to you about. The thing is that I'm dying to know what's up with P.A. You know Randy and I ran into her and this blond cutie up on Lovers' Leap. I just can't figure it out. I'm more curious about this than about anything that's happening on *General Hospital*. And I can't find out a thing. Alison's clamming up. Nobody else seems to know anything. And so I got this idea to do a little detective work. But I didn't want to ask Shelley. She's all wrapped up in the Glamour Queen these days. And Faith's too practical . . . and good. She'd think this was just a harebrained scheme . . . and not quite ethical maybe."

"And so you came to good old impractical, harebrained, unethical me," Casey chided.

"And so I came to the one person I know whose spirit of adventure always triumphs over her fear of getting caught."

Casey pulled a Snickers bar out of the pocket of her shorts, unwrapped it as she walked, and then broke it in two and passed a half over to Dana.

"Just what sort of scheme do you have in your antic little mind?" she asked Dana.

"Oh," Dana said, trying to sound casual, "just a little light eavesdropping."

"I know. You want us to hang upside-down from tree branches up at Lovers' Leap, in case they come walking by underneath. Dana, I don't think I'm in condition for this."

"You think you could manage to sit behind a bush?" Dana asked. "That's all I had in mind."

"This bush you speak of, O Mistress of Intrigue — it couldn't be under one of the windows of the abode of our illustrious head-mistress?"

"You're so perceptive, O Devoted Follower," Dana said.

"But how do we know when to get out there in the bush?" Casey asked.

"I've borrowed Ginny Weissberg's telescope. If I set it up on the roof at night, I can see all the way to P.A.'s house. I just look every night until I see The Guy in there, and then we get close enough to an open window to hear some of their conversation."

As Dana outlined her plan she felt an enormous wave of guilt. She knew what she was suggesting was really low, but her curiousity was overwhelming.

"Oh boy, I don't know," Casey said, tossing her crumpled candy wrapper into a trash basket, basketball-style. "If we get caught at this, we could be in big trouble."

"Casey," Dana said, pushing aside the guilt,

"I can't believe I'm hearing this. Don't tell me you're losing the old Flint nerves of steel."

Dana knew this would do the trick. Casey took pride in being bold. The thought of her reputation being diminished was enough to win her over to the idea.

"All right," she said. "I'll be your accomplice. I'm sort of curious myself about this. *Not* curious enough, though, to sit up on the roof with a telescope. You'll have to case the joint yourself. But I'll be on call. Come get me when the time is right and I'll be up in a flash."

"Spies together forever," Dana said, extending her hand.

Casey took and shook it, saying, "Until death, or getting caught by P.A." She thought a moment, then said, "I'm not sure which would be worse."

Dana hauled Ginny Weissberg's telescope up on the roof the next night and the night after that. Both nights P.A.'s house was dark. *She must be out for the evening,* Dana thought. She often went to dinner with friends, and frequently went down to Boston to go to movies or theater or dance performances. The third night, there *were* lights on in the living room, but from what Dana could see, P.A. was very much alone and reading a book. After an hour, Dana got too bored to go on. Watching someone read a book was about as exciting as watching paint dry. Though she didn't allow herself to deal with it, she also left because she felt so crummy about doing this.

The night after that, it was pouring rain and Dana didn't go up to the roof at all. She was about to forget the whole thing but then the very next night was clear, and when she looked into one of P.A.'s living room windows, the figure that went from blur to crisp was The Guy.

He wasn't just talking. He was standing in the middle of the living room, gesturing angrily. It looked like the words he was speaking were harsh ones.

Dana ran to Casey's room. Casey was sitting next to her stereo with her headset on, and so didn't hear Dana come in. Unfortunately, Maureen Gibson was there next to Casey, her nose stuck in a textbook on rock formations.

Maureen was an *extremely* serious girl. She already had her career as a geologist all planned. She knew what college and graduate school she would go to, and what area of research she would specialize in. She already knew who she would marry. She'd been going with some equally scientific guy from her hometown in New Jersey since they were both thirteen. They already knew what month in the year after they graduated from college they were going to get married. (Faith had commented sarcastically on hearing this that they probably already had a deposit on the reception hall.)

Everyone was amazed that Maureen and

Casey got along so well. Dana thought it must be a case of opposites complementing each other.

"Hi, Maureen," Dana said to her now. She lifted her eyes from her book for a split second and grunted something that was probably her version of "Hi," then went back to her rock formations.

Dana walked over to the corner, hunkered down next to Casey and pulled her earphones off.

"Like to take a little walk with me?" she said.

"Oh, thanks anyway, Dana, but I'm in the middle of this heavy Van Halen tape. I think I'll just stay here and groove."

"Oh, no, Case," Dana said, giving her a pinch, "I think what you really want is a little walk." To make sure she was getting her message across, she gave a heavy wink.

"Ah!" Casey said, like a cartoon character with a light bulb going on over its head. "*That* little walk. Oh, of course. I'm *dying*, simply dying for some fresh air."

"Reeny," she said, "Dana and I are going for a little stroll."

"Mmmrrmmph," Maureen said. It was her all-purpose grunt.

Casey and Dana slipped past her, out the door. When they got down the hall a ways, Casey asked, "What's up?"

"He's there!" Dana said, tugging excitedly on Casey's arm. "Come on. We've got to hurry.

It looked like they were having a real turbulent conversation."

The two of them sprinted across campus.

"If anyone sees us," Dana shouted back to Casey, "they'll just think we're jogging."

"They'll probably think we've just robbed the payroll office. We'll probably get ten to twenty in maximum security, but that's okay. What're friends for, I say."

When they got close to Patrice Allardyce's house, they slowed to a walk, trying to look casual, as if they were just out for a stroll.

"Without being obvious about it," Dana said, "let's try to see where the action is, so we know which window to get under."

But although there were lights on in the main floor windows, there was no sign of either Patrice or The Guy. They couldn't stop because a group of girls was passing them, apparently on their way back from seeing a movie or getting ice cream in Greenleaf. And then coming down the path the other way was Ms. Selby, the gym teacher, walking with Mr. Gray, who taught biology at Oakley Prep, the boys school down the road. The rumor was that they were an "item." They had barely passed when Casey tugged on Dana's t-shirt.

"Come on. Let's make a run for the house." Casey noticed Dana looking toward the two teachers. "Come on. They're too goony over each other to notice us. If we don't make a break for it someone else'll just come along."

"Casey," Dana said, "maybe we should just

go back to our rooms. Forget the whole thing."

"Dana," Casey said, "you started this and we're going to finish it."

And so the two of them — Casey first, with Dana close behind — took off toward the house. At the last minute, Dana took a running roll into a clump of bushes underneath one of the big living room windows. Casey was so close behind that when she took her roll, she landed right on top of Dana.

"Mmmrrmmphh," Dana grunted, swallowing a large "Ouch!"

"Did I hurt you?" Casey whispered.

"In about six places, I think. It's okay. I'll probably live. At least we got here without getting spotted."

"Yeah, but where are we? I don't hear anything. How are we going to eavesdrop if they're not here?"

"Well, they're here somewhere. We'll just have to go around the house until we find them."

"Maybe they left."

"No, Case. Both cars are in the driveway."

It was hard getting around the house. They either had to crawl around through the bushes and shrubs that bordered the house, or, where there were gaps, they had to make fast little runs, hoping no one passing on any of the nearby campus paths saw them.

When they got to the back of the house, just before they turned the corner into the backyard, Dana stopped Casey abruptly.

"Shhhhhh," she said, covering Casey's mouth with her hand, even though Casey hadn't yet said anything.

"What?" Casey said, prying the hand off.

"Voices," Dana whispered. "Listen."

Sure enough, drifting in from around the corner were two muted voices — a man's and a woman's.

"We've got to get in closer," Casey said, "or we won't be able to hear what they're saying. I'll go first. I've done more skulduggery than you."

Dana sat with her back against the brick wall of the house, trembling slightly, her arm propped up on a drainspout. Suddenly, from the end of the spout emerged a frog.

Dana hated frogs. She thought they were the most repulsive creatures on earth — well, next to anteaters, but she had only seen photos of those. Sitting here in the dark, already a bundle of nerve endings, seeing this frog pop out of the end of the drainspout was all she needed to put her over the edge.

For one brief second, she forgot that the most important thing in the world was that she keep quiet. For one brief second, all she could think of was how disgustingly icky this slimy little frog was, and how close it was to her arm. For one split second, all she could do was jump about three feet in the air and give out with a scream.

Within an instant, Casey was back, out of breath.

"What happened!?" she whispered hoarsely.

"Frog," Dana said meekly, pointing at the now-empty end of the drainpipe. "Did they hear?"

"Of course they heard," Casey said, exasperated. "I'm sure everyone within a mile radius heard. But it only stopped their conversation for a second. I guess P.A.'s used to girl screams as a part of her general background noise. You know, like people in cities who live above the subway. They just get used to it."

"Where are they?" Dana said.

"On the back porch," Casey said. "This is going to be tough. The porch is really just a screened-in patio, you know. There's only one clump of bushes near it. It's the only place where we can both have cover *and* be able to hear what they're saying."

"What does it look like they're saying?" Dana asked.

"Well, they're not fighting anymore. Whatever they're talking about, they're saying it in real low tones. So we're going to have to get pretty close. It looks like a pretty serious, juicy conversation. I mean it doesn't look like he's the guy who's come to try to sell her a water softener."

"Should we do this?" Dana asked.

"Of course. Follow me," Casey said, and led the way.

They moved *very* slowly this time. They didn't want to be fast-moving objects that P.A. would notice out of the corner of her eye.

They were trying to be just a slightly moving part of the lawn. It seemed to take forever for them to reach the clump of bushes by the side of the porch.

Once there, Dana got more frightened than ever. They were so close to P.A. and The Guy that they could have almost reached out and touched them, if there weren't a screen between them. She couldn't say anything to Casey. There was no whisper soft enough to risk.

By the same token, though, they could hear every word of the conversation, as if they were on the porch with P.A. and her friend.

And he definitely did seem to be a friend of some kind. A close friend. The conversation they were having could only take place between people who knew each other very well, and for quite a long time.

The Guy was sitting on the sofa. He didn't look like he belonged there. He was wearing old jeans and a t-shirt with the sleeves rolled up. He had on old, beat-up cowboy boots. The couch was white rattan with cushions in a pretty blue and white paisley print. He looked like a fish out of water. Or a bull in a china shop.

Even his gestures and way of sitting were out of place there. He was hunkered over, his arms resting on his thighs, his hands clasped. His head was bent down, his long blond hair falling in his face. He looked serious and brooding.

Patrice Allardyce looked pretty serious herself. She was sitting across from him in a matching rattan chair. Although she looked much more like she belonged in this setting, she was definitely less cool, calm, and collected than the girls were used to seeing her. She had on white summer pants and a turquoise cotton shirt. She was leaning back in her chair, her feet propped up on the small coffee table between them. She was fidgeting nervously, picking small pieces off the rattan arm of her chair with the fingers of her right hand.

Dana and Casey had clearly come in in the middle of a tense moment.

"But how could you just abandon me like that?" he was saying, a pleading tone in his voice.

"I didn't *just abandon* you," P.A. said sarcastically. "I tried a hundred times to show you I cared, to try to make a difference. But nothing I did worked. You didn't *want* my help then."

"But when I did," he said, "you turned your back on me."

"I had to, Yale," she said, looking down, not at him.

"Do you know how lonely it is in prison?" he asked her in a sad, low voice.

"Do you know what it would've done to my career to be linked with you then? Oh Yale, I couldn't save you, so I had to save myself. But honey, if you knew how much I missed you through that time. I was counting the days and months as if *I* were the prisoner."

"Patsy," he said, getting up. "I just can't listen to this anymore. If you'd really loved me, you would've been there."

On this note, he stormed out the back door of the porch and tromped out into the dark yard. In the process, he stepped squarely with one of his large cowboy boots on the hand of one Dana Morrison, Girl Detective.

Thankfully, Girl Accomplice, Casey Flint, was fast enough to put a hand over the wailing mouth of her friend so that her scream of pain went unheard by anyone. And then, when Patrice Allardyce had run after her friend into the woods adjoining her backyard, Casey got Dana up on her feet and took her back to the dorm.

Sitting on the edge of a sink in the fourth floor bathroom of Baker, her hand in the washbowl, which Casey had filled with ice cubes sneaked out of the cafeteria, Dana finally moaned out loud.

"This is what I get for being so rotten. I think I'm wounded for life," Dana said.

"No. You can move your hand. That's got to be a good sign. But if it's still bad tomorrow, we'll get you down to see good old Zenger, Killer Nurse."

"Oh no! Not that! Anything but that! I'll get better. I promise."

Actually Nurse Zenger was able and caring and nice, but she had an unfortunately witch-like appearance that had gotten her a reputation — completely made up by years of Canby girls — for cures made with bat wings and eye of newt, and potions brewed up at midnight in her smoking cauldron.

"Well," Casey said, sitting on the tile floor next to Dana, eating an Eskimo Pie from the machines in the basement, "even if you lose the hand, it was worth it. Can you believe what we heard?"

"He was in *prison!*" Dana said, sadly.

"And if she'd loved him enough, she would've stuck with him, even though she was a swanky headmistress and he was a jailbird," Casey said.

"But you know," Dana said, "the part that makes the pain in my hand feel like almost nothing and my guilt over eavesdropping almost disappear?"

"What?" Casey said, her mouth full of ice cream.

"Finding out that there's someone in this world who actually calls Patrice Allardyce PATSY!"

CHAPTER TEN

Shelley was blowdrying her hair in front of the mirror over the dresser in 407. Dana came up behind her and stared at Shelley's reflection. Shelley turned off the dryer.

"This is how you do it now?" Dana asked. "Without a brush?"

"Mmmmhmm. The guy who cut it for me back home this summer showed me this. You put the blower on low, then just keep running your fingers through it as it dries. The idea is to get it all wild and full and tangly." She turned and looked hard at Dana's hair, lifting a heavy handful of it. "I don't think it would work for you. Yours is too straight."

"I know," Dana said, eyeing herself in the mirror. "Do you think I should get a permanent?"

"I think if you do, you should go to a salon to get it. I gave myself one at home a couple of years ago and spent a whole summer looking like I'd stuck my finger in an electric socket."

"Where're you going tonight?" Dana asked.

"Tom mowed about a hundred lawns this week, so he's taking me for a pizza. What time is it?"

"Six-thirty," Dana said, looking at her black runner's watch.

"Why am I always ready half an hour early?" Shelley wondered. "I mean girls in movies are always keeping the guys waiting. Not me. I'll bet I've spent at least a tenth of my teen-age years sitting around waiting for guys. Either waiting for them to call, or waiting for them to come by." She sighed. "I guess I might as well wait out front. It's probably one of the last really nice nights we'll have before the October monsoons hit."

Shelley brought her French verb cards down with her and laid them out on the stone bench she was sitting on. She had her eyes closed, memorizing the past tenses — the *passé composé* and the *imparfait* — of the verb *savoir* — to know — when she heard a sarcastic voice directly above her say, "What are you doing, chanting your mantra or something?"

Shelley opened her eyes and looked up.

"Hi, Pamela," she said.

"You waiting for someone?" Pamela asked. "Your darling roommates?" Since the ill-fated dinner at the Auberge, Pamela's mild contempt for Faith and Dana had turned to intense dislike. Shelley tried hard not to bring them up in conversation. She didn't want to have to hear what Pamela would say about them, and didn't want to fight with Pamela over them.

Now when they got together, it was mostly in Pamela's room. This was okay. More than okay in some ways. Pamela had a huge stereo with a collection of about a thousand great records. She also had a huge color tv *and* video recorder. Every month, her mother sent a package of movie cassettes. So a lot of nights, Shelley ran down to the student center for popcorn, while Pamela pulled the blinds and set up all the pillows and bolsters on the floor and popped in a cassette of one of the latest movies and they'd watch and talk and laugh. Pamela had seen most movies in private screening rooms rather than in theaters, and so had gotten used to delivering a running commentary — usually sarcastic — as the film ran. Shelley thought it was fun watching with her.

Lately, though, Shelley was beginning to realize that a big reason she liked watching movies with Pamela was that it gave them a way of being together without having to really talk, of being friends without really building any connection between them.

The thing was, she didn't really want to talk much with Pamela, or find out more about her. Almost everything she had found out so far just made her sad, and made her feel farther and farther away from Pamela.

It seemed that for Pamela, everything broke down into two categories — things that were interesting because they were what, or who, Pamela wanted at the moment; or things that were stupid, which was everything and everybody else. These people and things were laughable.

For instance, French was the *only* language to study. Everything else was just a waste of time. Especially Latin. Nobody even spoke it anymore. Pamela thought girls who signed up to take Latin shouldn't be given sharp objects like knives and forks in the dining room. They were clearly too dumb to manage them and might hurt themselves. She called dumb kids, and she put almost every girl at Canby Hall in this category, "The Spoon Set."

And all boys were dopes, except Bret Harper. And days when he didn't call her — there were more and more of those, it seemed to Shelley — even *he* was a dope.

This kind of attitude made Shelley uncomfortable. It seemed so self-centered and negative. But she was too intimidated by Pamela to contradict her. And so she usually sat silent, listening but not agreeing.

But when they just watched movies, she didn't have all these problems with Pamela.

Shelley's view of Pamela had changed a lot from those first days of knowing her. Now instead of being snowed, Shelley felt sorry for her. She *did* know all those stars, but not that well, and when she got to talking about them, she was just as critical as she was of kids around here.

She didn't seem to have any close friends. She never got any calls or letters from kids back home. She didn't talk about missing anybody.

When Casey had asked Shelley a week or so before why she hung out with Pamela, Shelley had had to admit, "I think if I didn't, she wouldn't have anyone around here to be with. Most of the girls didn't like her to begin with. And she's bad-mouthed most of the ones who were sort of on her side at first. Plus, she really likes me. She doesn't show it a lot, but I know I'm important to her. I think maybe I'm her first friend. Really. You don't want to drop somebody if you're their only friend in the world."

Tonight, Pamela was looking forlorn.

"What's the matter?" Shelley asked her, putting away her flash cards. She didn't want Pamela helping her with her French, something she always wanted to do to show off how good she was at it.

"Oh, I'm just dragged. Bret's apparently gone home for a week. Back to Boston. His roommate told me when I called today. Odd he didn't say anything to me before he left."

"It is," Shelley said, not mentioning that she had seen him crossing the campus not ten minutes ago with Natalie Fenton.

Pamela sighed and sat down on the bench where the flashcards had been.

"What are you doing tonight? You want to go to the Auberge with me? My treat, of course."

"Thanks, but Tom's coming by," Shelley said. "We're going to Pizza Pete's."

Pamela didn't say anything, just sat there. Shelley could only take a minute of this heavy silence before she heard herself saying, "I know! Why don't you come along!"

"Oh, I couldn't," Pamela said. "I mean it's *your* date and all."

"No, really, it's not that much of a date. Tom and I see each other all the time. And he's been wanting to meet you anyway."

This was not exactly true. Actually, it was a complete lie. From Shelley's descriptions of Pamela, Tom had come to his own conclusions about her.

"She sounds like trouble," was his estimate.

And so she knew he was probably not going to be wild with happiness when he found out she had just invited Pamela along.

"Well, if you're *really* sure it's okay," Pamela said coyly.

"Really," Shelley said.

"Then I'll just go up and change into something more devastating. You never know who you're going to run into in that pulsing metropolis of Greenleaf on a Saturday night."

"But Pamela, you look fine like you are. Besides, Tom's due here in five minutes and he goes crazy when people are late."

"I won't be a minute," Pamela said, getting

up. "And if I am, it'll do him good to wait for once. Really, Michelle, you have to learn how to train a boy."

When she was gone, Shelley sat back down on the bench with a sigh and got out her verb cards again. Ten minutes later, Tom came strolling up. Twenty minutes after that, Pamela came strolling down.

By this time, Tom was furious — with Shelley for inviting Pamela along on their date, without even checking with him first, and with Pamela for keeping them waiting.

By the time she got back down, they were sitting side by side on the bench in silence. Tom was steaming and Shelley wondering how she could have been stupid enough to get herself into this mess.

Everything changed, though, when Pamela arrived. She was wearing a bright blue cotton sweater, and pleated khakis. It looked like she had washed and freshly redone her hair. It looked like a shampoo ad. She had put on so much cologne spray that Shelley half expected to see a cloud of vapors around her.

Really, Pam, we're just going for a pizza, not to the prom, was Shelley's first thought. Then she looked over and caught the expression on Tom's face. He was looking at Pamela like he had never seen a girl before.

"Hi," she said, but it wasn't a regular hi. It was more like the sound butter makes melting on pancakes. And it wasn't directed to both Tom and Shelley. Her eyes were glued to his. It was as if Shelley had disappeared.

"Sorry I'm late. I just couldn't bear to meet you looking like I'd just been washing my dog."

This didn't seem like an especially funny joke to Shelley, but Tom laughed like he was watching a Steve Martin movie.

"It's okay," he said. "You're not that late. And it gave us a chance to sit out here and enjoy the night."

Shelley looked at him like he was crazy, but he didn't see this. He appeared to be hypnotized by Pamela.

Tom had his dad's car and he ushered them over to it.

"This way, ladies," he said with an uncharacteristic flourish of his hand.

"Oh sir," Pamela sighed, like a swooning belle out of some movie about the Deep South. "You are so kind."

Shelley thought she might throw up.

When they got to the car, Shelley opened the door on her side, and pulled down the front seat, both to put an end to this chivalry joke, and to show Pamela that, cute as she was, her place on this date was in the backseat.

A little before Pamela was all the way in, Shelley gave the seat a swift slam back into Pamela's hip.

"Ooops, sorry," she said, sarcastically at first. Then when she saw the hurt expression on Pamela's face, she really *was* sorry. She was probably being paranoid. Here her good friend was trying to be sociable with her boyfriend, and she was acting like Pamela was trying to get Tom to elope with her tonight. *Calm down*, she told herself.

No sooner were they on their way than Pamela pushed her head and shoulders through the space between Tom and Shelley.

"Hi you two," she said cheerily. "I was getting lonesome back here."

"Then I'll put on the rear speakers," Tom said. "Just sit back and relax." He flipped a switch on the dashboard and then dropped his hand onto Shelley's. She looked at him. He was smiling. Now she felt doubly foolish for having suspected anything going on between him and Pamela.

They drove the rest of the way into town listening to the car radio.

When they got to Pizza Pete's, the place was nearly full, but Tom found an empty booth near the back. Shelley slid in on one side, Pamela on the other. Without hesitation, Tom slid in next to Shelley.

"Shelley tells me you're on the swim team at Greenleaf," Pamela said to Tom. Shelley noticed that there was none of the usual sarcastic tone in her voice tonight. She sounded like a completely different person.

"Yeah," Tom said. He was modest about being the top man on the team. "Shelley and I are practically porpoises, given how much time we've spent in the water. Of course, this year, she's given that up. Out of the pool and onto the stage."

"When are your meets?" Pamela asked.

"I'd love to come." She was leaning practically across the table as she said this.

At this point, Shelley had to concede that Pamela's interest in Tom was *not* interest in him as Shelley's boyfriend, that she was not just being friendly. She was clearly making a play for him.

Shelley felt utterly betrayed. She had put up with Pamela's outrageous behavior, stood by her when no one else would, and this was what she got in return. She had to admit now that Faith and Dana had probably been right all along. Pamela's glamour was only skin deep, and underneath she was a really rotten person.

She didn't know what to do. Her face was hot with anger. She didn't think there was any way she could get through this charade of an evening. And yet, she couldn't think of any way to get out of it at this point.

"Excuse me," she said, giving Tom a little nudge. "I'd like to go to the ladies' room." He slid out and let her pass by. All she could think of was getting away for a few minutes to think over what to do.

Once inside the ladies' room, Shelley turned on the cold water full blast. She bent over the washbowl and splashed it onto her face until the hot feeling went away.

She looked at herself in the mirror. She looked pretty terrible — like someone who has just received some very bad news. Like the character on one of the soaps who has just learned that her husband has embezzled a million dollars from the bank where he works.

I look sick, she thought, then realized she could use this to her advantage. She could go back out and plead a sudden case of flu, and ask Tom for a lift back to the dorm. That way she wouldn't have to make a scene over this.

She couldn't tell for sure how Tom was responding to this flirting. He seemed flattered by Pamela's interest, but she didn't think he was really falling for it. The main thing was that Shelley trusted him. Of course, she had trusted Pamela, too. Maybe she was just a rotten judge of character.

She was so confused she couldn't think straight right now. All she knew was that she had to put a stop to this stupid dinner now. Later, she could call Tom and tell him the truth.

Feeling that she now had the situation at least minimally under control, she went back into the restaurant. It wasn't until she got nearly up to the booth that she saw that Pamela had moved from her side of the table over to Tom's and was sitting practically smashed up against him, holding his hand. The worst of it was that he didn't seem to be fighting it at all.

At this point, Shelley lost every ounce of cool she had. She rushed past the two of them and ran out of the restaurant and kept going all the way down Main — past where the stores ended and the houses began. Soon after that, she heard fast, hard footsteps following her.

"Shel!" Tom's voice shouted after her. "Shelley, stop! Please!"

She slowed down, then stopped, then turned around as Tom rushed up to her. For a minute or so, all he could do was stand there panting. When he caught his breath enough to speak, he said, "Shel. What did you think was going on back there? Do you think all guys are just dopes who fall for girls who flirt outrageously enough? Come on. She's cute. I can't deny that. But you're my girl. I'm not looking for any new ones this week. And even if I were, I wouldn't be interested in someone who was dripping all that fake attention all over me like honey. Yuk."

"Well, that's what I thought," Shelley said through her tears. "Until I saw you holding hands like lovebirds."

"What was I going to do?" he pleaded. "No sooner were you gone than she practically jumped across the table and started telling me how she could tell fortunes and she was going to read my palm. I mean, she's *your* friend. I was really just trying to be a sociable guy. Honest." He stopped here and looked at Shelley with such a direct, straightforward gaze that she knew he was telling the truth.

"Okay," Shelley said. "Explanation accepted. You can't blame me for jumping to the wrong conclusion, though."

"What I think you ought to do," Tom said, taking both of her hands in his, "is jump away from *that* particular friend. As they say, with friends like that. . . ."

"I know," Shelley said, nodding thoughtfully, "you don't need enemies."

CHAPTER ELEVEN

"You just left her there in Pizza Pete's?!" Dana burst out laughing.

"I'd love to have seen her expression," Faith said. "She's so cute when she's mad."

"Come on, you two," Shelley pleaded. "I didn't mean to leave her there. I was just so upset over what had happened in Pete's, and then Tom came running after me and calmed me down, but we were so deep into talking about us by the time we got back to his car that I just got in and we headed back. It wasn't until we got to the campus that I remembered that we'd left Pamela in the pizzeria. We turned around and drove back, but by that time, of course, she was gone. I know she's a rotten person, but *I'm* not. I really wouldn't have left her there, as little as I think of her now."

"I know," Dana said, hopping from her bed onto Shelley's and putting a consoling arm over her friend's shoulder. "But there is a sort of poetic justice to that wart making such a big play for Tom, then winding up sitting there all by herself looking like a complete fool. I'm so glad you finally realized how awful she is. I think it's important that we three have other friends, but this one was a definite strain on our friendship. So I can't say I'm sorry you've decided to drop her."

"But you'll be seeing her soon," Faith said. She was on the floor, doing the push-up part of her nightly aerobic workout.

"*Never* would be too soon as far as I'm concerned," Shelley said. "I was pretty near the end of my rope with her anyway, but tonight really did it. My friendship is valuable. I'm not about to squander it on anyone who cares so little about me in return."

"I agree," Faith said. "I understand that you don't ever want to see Ms. Young again, but *she'll* be needing to get in a last word. Just be prepared. You'll be able to handle it."

Faith's advice came in handy later that night, when the door to 407 pushed open without anyone knocking first. It was Pamela. She was holding a pizza box, which she deliberately dropped on the floor in front of her.

She glared at Shelley and said, "You forgot your dinner." Then she turned and stalked out.

The three roommates sat for a moment in stunned silence until Faith, in her most fake innocent voice said, "My, my. Such a surly delivery person. I guess it really *is* hard to get good help these days."

CHAPTER TWELVE

Shelley was nervous. This was the first read-through of the fall production of the Canby Hall drama club. The play was called "Blarney" and was about life among Irish peat farmers.

Ms. MacPherson, the drama coach who was known as Ms. Mac, loved plays set in Ireland, or written by Irish playwrights. This one seemed pretty dull to Shelley, but she wanted to do well in it. She was playing the younger sister of the lead character, a young man who wants to leave the peat bogs and move to Dublin and get into computers.

Ms. Mac hadn't been around the past summer to see Shelley shine in the acting intensive given by André Rosofsky, the famous New York acting coach. And so Shelley was going to have to impress her now. She held onto her script with a sweaty hand while Jack Farnsworth, a senior from Oakley

Prep who had the lead in the play, read a long line of his.

"But Rose, can't you see I'm tired of havin' these here callouses on me hands, of workin' from sun to sun. . . ."

He had quite a ways to go before it would be Shelley's turn to read her line. She grew distracted while waiting. She loved being on this stage, which was nearly as old as the school. She loved thinking of all the plays that had been put on there. She wondered what the plays performed in 1912, or 1927, or even 1963, had been like. She'd love to have seen them.

She thought of all those hundreds of thousands of lines delivered by girls now grown up, some grown old, some no longer even living. All of them up there on the stage with its worn, but highly polished floorboards, its heavy, purple, velvet curtain, its long row of brilliant footlights. It was thrilling being up there, even just during rehearsals. She knew being on a stage was where she wanted to be. And she was willing to study and work hard for as many years as it would take for her to make it as an actress.

"Shelley! Shelley!" Ms. Mac was shouting from the back of the darkened theater. "Could we interrupt your train of thought for just a moment so you can speak your line?"

Shelley felt herself blushing. How could she have let herself drift off so far that she had missed her cue entirely?

She quickly found her place and read, in

her best Irish brogue, "Oh Sean, but you can't be leavin' us. What'll the family do without ya? You're the best peat man in all the county."

"No! No! No!" came disembodied shouts from the back. With the lights out in the auditorium, it was impossible to see Ms. Mac, which made her comments doubly scary. She went on, "This play is supposed to be set in Ireland, not in Brooklyn. Or Tuscaloosa. Or Dallas. Or wherever that accent comes from."

"Sorry, Ms. Mac. I'll try again." Shelley felt humiliated.

"This time just read it without an accent. We can work on your brogue later. It seemed much better to me during auditions. Maybe because you were trying then."

Shelley read the line, but felt defeated and down on herself for not having really worked on her brogue the night before. She also felt angry with Ms. Mac for embarrassing her in front of the rest of the cast. She worried that now Mac was going to ride her for the rest of the rehearsals. She might have heard that Shelley had been a star during the summer and wanted to whittle her down a few pegs. This might, of course, be entirely a figment of Shelley's own imagination, but she worried just the same.

After rehearsal, she ducked going for Cokes with a bunch of the kids from the cast. She felt too crummy. She just shuffled back to Baker, kicking the first few leaves that had fallen onto the campus paths.

By the time she got back to the room, she had not calmed down at all; rather she had worked herself up into a pretty bad state about her future as an actress. She was hoping Faith or Dana would be around to talk to. There were some times a girl especially needed her roommates.

But the room was empty. She saw from the digital alarm clock next to Dana's floor mattress bed that it was past six. Rehearsal had run on a long time apparently. Then she saw a message scrawled in lipstick on the mirror by the door — one of the main forms of communication in 407. The messages and shades of lipstick changed from day to day, but there was almost always something scrawled there. Today it said:

WAITED UNTIL NEAR STARVATION. MEET US IN D.R.

That meant the dining room, but Shelley didn't feel like eating. She was too down in the dumps. She tried to think of something that would cheer her up, but she couldn't.

"Might as well get something done," she said aloud to herself. It was her old reliable cure for a bad mood — doing some objectionable task. Usually the satisfaction of having done something difficult picked up her spirits. She didn't need to think long to come up with her most objectionable task — writing her paper on the reign of Charlemagne for her European history class.

"Argh," she said, just thinking of how much she didn't want to write this paper. But there was clearly no time like the present, and so she got out her research books from the library, her yellow legal pad full of notes, and her box of typing paper.

There was only one typewriter in 407. It belonged to Dana, but all three of them used it. Shelley looked around now and spotted it on Faith's desk. There was a sheet of paper already rolled into it. Shelley sat down and, without really thinking, started to read. It was clearly a letter from Faith to her older sister Sarah, who was in college at Georgetown.

Dear Sis, (*Shelley smiled. She wouldn't have guessed that Faith would call her sister anything as corny as "Sis."*)

Things have been pretty boring around here lately, Sarah. Sometimes I wonder if this is the right place for me. I have a hard time finding anyone I like. Most of the kids here are just so nowhere. Even my roommates.

Oh, I guess Dana's all right, if you don't mind hanging out with someone whose main intellectual interest is clothes. (*Shelley couldn't believe Faith felt like this. She thought Faith was crazy about Dana.*)

But Shelley's simply impossible. Remember when I first got here and didn't like her at all? Well, I'm beginning to think I was right after all, that I should've trusted my first impression.

If she was insufferable when she was just off that farm, she's worse now. Now she thinks she's an actress, a great lady of the "theatah," if you know what I mean. Goes around all the time sounding like Sarah Bernhardt or something. Give me a break. I saw her as Cordelia in the summer intensive show and I'm telling you that if you put that girl in a paper bag, she could not act her way out of it.

The letter stopped here. Not that Shelley could have stood to read any more of this anyway. She put her head down on the desk and began to cry.

When Dana and Faith came up from dinner, they were laughing all the way down the hall, and then fell all over each other — still laughing — onto their beds.

"Sue Murphy slipped on a pea," Dana was finally able to get out between new waves of laughter.

"It wasn't really funny, but it really was, if you know what I mean," Faith said.

"Yeah," Dana said, wiping her tears with the back of her hand. "She was hurrying over to her table with a full tray. She'd just come out of the line and was headed toward her table. Then all of a sudden, there was this little pea on the floor. . . ."

Faith picked up the story from there.

"And unsuspecting Sue takes a surfin' safari. She must've sailed about ten feet. She never fell — just kept cruising along. Everything was flying off her tray — beets, gravy, tapioca. She finally slowed down and found a handy wall to stop her."

"At first she looked like she was going to die of embarrassment," Dana said. "But then she got into it and started laughing along with everyone else."

The two of them were so wrapped up in their hilarity that they didn't notice for a while that Shelley was not amused — was, in fact, staring hard at the history book on the desk in front of her. She wasn't looking up at them at all.

Dana was the first to see the problem.

"Hey! What's up, Shelleroodles? How can studying be more fascinating than Sue Murphy taking a skid on a pea?"

Shelley still didn't say anything. She just picked the letter up from her desk and held it aloft, as far away from herself as she could — as if it were an old piece of cheese.

"What's that?" Faith asked.

"You ought to know," Shelley said. "I found it in the typewriter on your desk when I went to type my paper. I believe you are the only person in this room with a sister named Sarah."

Faith took the letter and read it. Dana came up behind her and read over her shoulder.

When she was finished, Faith looked up and told both of them, "I didn't write this."

"Yeah, sure," Shelley spat out. "I suppose some little gremlin did, then? Or maybe an interplanetary visitor from a saucer that just landed on the roof? Faith — this is to *your* sister. I found it on *your* desk. How could you be such a phony — pretending to like me, to be my friend when you really feel like this! You're rotten. You really are."

With that, she ripped the letter out of Faith's hand, crumpled it into a tight ball, and threw it hard at Faith, then turned, and ran out of the room.

Faith turned to Dana, eyes wide with concern. "You don't think I wrote that, do you?"

Dana couldn't look Faith in the eyes. "I don't know *what* to think. I mean the letter is there and. . . ."

Faith just stared at Dana. "I can understand Shelley's reaction. She's like that. She just lets all her instant feelings hang out, without thinking things through. But you . . . you're different. You stop and think before you accuse."

Dana felt tears coming to her eyes. "I . . . you're right. There must be an explanation." But deep inside, Dana wasn't sure there was; wasn't sure Faith hadn't written the letter, and she couldn't bear the thought.

CHAPTER THIRTEEN

Faith was in the photo darkroom of the *Canby Clarion*, the school paper. She was printing up a roll of pictures she had taken of Shelley at the beginning of the term. It was two days since Shelley had found the letter, and she still had not spoken to Faith. Dana was just keeping her distance and being pointedly cool. So developing this roll of film and printing it up was the only way Faith could think of to make some kind of connection with her roommate.

With her tongs, Faith prodded the blank rectangle of paper around in the developing solution until the picture began to come up.

In taking the picture, Faith had positioned herself at the end of the school pool and had Shelley do the butterfly, then caught her head-on as she burst out of the water like a fish in midocean. It was a great shot. And it so captured Shelley's energy. Faith felt sad just looking at this picture of a friend she had apparently lost. She felt alone and terribly misunderstood.

She *hadn't* written the letter. It was someone's idea of a practical joke. But what a cruel joke. How was she ever going to get Shelley and Dana to believe she hadn't done it? And who had?

Her reverie was broken by a sharp knock on the door.

"Can I come in?" Marylou Wilson shouted from outside. She was the editor of the *Clarion*.

"No. I'm developing," Faith shouted back. "I'll be out pretty soon, though."

"You don't have to," Marylou said. "I just wanted to relay a message. Shelley called. She wants you to meet her out by the falls in half an hour. She says it's important."

"Okay, thanks," Faith said, looking down at the now fully developed print of Shelley, at first smiling at the thought of getting this mess straightened out. Then the smile gave way to a look of worry.

Half an hour, she thought. *That's when I'm supposed to meet Johnny. I'll just have to call and tell him something really important has come up.*

Johnny wasn't happy about being stood up.

"Oh no," he groaned. "I haven't seen you in days. I miss my girl. You and your friends are always having one crisis or another. Can't you miss one crisis so you can be with your boyfriend?"

"Please understand," Faith said. "She thinks I betrayed her. I thought she might never speak to me again. If she's willing to talk, I've got to go out there."

"Okay," Johnny said and sighed. "But this means I get a double date tomorrow. We go to two movies and have two sodas afterward, and I get two kisses at the door."

Faith laughed. "It's a deal," she said.

Faith hated to miss seeing Johnny this afternoon. Especially this afternoon. Today was his birthday. He didn't know she knew. His mother had told her. Early this morning, before classes, Faith had used the kitchenette in Alison's apartment and baked him a little cake. It was going to be a surprise. Well, so much for that.

Still, some things were more important than dates or birthdays. Friendships for instance. And if she had a chance to save this one, she wasn't going to pass it up.

As she was walking out Old Fort Road, Faith began to wonder why Shelley wanted them to meet way out at the falls. Why not on campus, or in Greenleaf? The falls were a long hike. Faith was going to have to run half the way to make it in time.

When she got there, the falls were completely deserted. This was a summer gathering spot for Canby girls and Oakley boys and kids from Greenleaf High. But summer was being replaced by fall now. Today, there was a slight nip in the air. Not cold really, just chilly enough to make you button your sweater and roll your sleeves down.

Still, it was kind of nice being out here when no one else was, Faith thought. She was surprised she had beaten Shelley out here. Shelley was the most on-time person in the world. Dana and Faith always kidded her about it. Shelley thought being either late or early were impolite. If she had, for instance, told Casey she'd be by to get her for a movie at seven, and arrived at 6:57, she would stand outside Casey's door and wait three minutes before knocking. So it was odd that she wasn't here yet.

Still, if Faith had to be waiting anywhere, the falls were the prettiest place she could think of — especially with the late afternoon shafts of sunlight shooting through the thinning leaves on the trees, making dancing lights on the rushing water.

Faith hopped out across the stream, from rock to rock, until she came to the big flat one in the middle. The sun was pouring down on this spot and, although the day was cool, there it was warm as summer. So warm that after a few minutes, she peeled off both her jacket and sweater, and after a few minutes, lay down on the rock and feel asleep.

She awoke, thinking someone had taken her blanket away and then realized she wasn't in bed and that the missing blanket was the sun, which had now sunk behind the trees. She looked at her watch. Nearly five. She'd been asleep for over an hour.

She sat up and looked around. She was still the only living soul in sight. Shelley had apparently never shown up.

A rush of emotions surged through Faith. First, she was simply bewildered that Shelley hadn't shown up. Where could she be? Had Faith gotten the message wrong?

No. She knew she hadn't. And suddenly her bewilderment turned to hurt. Why didn't Shelley want to see her? But she *had* wanted to. It was Shelley who had wanted to see Faith. In a flash it was clear to Faith that she had been set up. Shelley had misled her to get her to the falls — away from the darkroom, away from her birthday treat for Johnny — and then she had deliberately not shown up.

How could she!? The creep. Now Faith was good and mad. She leaped up and took the little rocks two at a time until she was on the bank. She ran up it and through the woods to the road and kept on running for half a mile. *I'll tell that girl off, but good*, she thought as she ran.

Then, as she began to get winded and slowed down, her thoughts changed. Why bother telling Shelley off? Why give her the satisfaction of a big scene? It would be much better not to say a thing. That would drive Shelley crazy. She'd have to wonder why Faith wasn't mad. She'd have to think maybe

Faith hadn't shown up at the falls either — that she, Shelley, had been the one who'd been stood up.

Faith laughed to herself as she thought of this. It was a stroke of genius, if she had to admit it herself.

I'll never talk to her again . . . about anything.

CHAPTER FOURTEEN

The next morning was Wednesday, which meant Room Check. Sometime during morning classes, Alison would inspect all the rooms in Baker, holding her clipboard with her checklist of twenty-five points of tidiness, neatness, and cleanliness that every room should possess.

407 never possessed all twenty-five. Not once in all the weeks and months of Room Checks had Dana, Faith, and Shelley gotten a perfect score. Actually, they hadn't gotten anywhere near a perfect score. Usually, they had around a fifteen. Sometimes lower. Once they got an eleven. They were always among the ten worst rooms in the dorm.

And they couldn't understand it. They all thought they really tried to keep the place together. They hung their clothes up and swept the floor and got rid of all their old milk cartons and Coke cups.

But they didn't always miss on the same

points. Some weeks it was that they'd forgotten to empty the wastebasket. Others it was that they hadn't dusted their desks and bookshelves.

There was almost always a problem with their beds, though. Right from the start, they had put their bedframes down in storage so they could have islandlike floor mattresses, covered with pastel spreads and lots of pillows. Unfortunately, this kind of bed did not lend itself to proper making, Canby-style.

Canby-style was with the sheet and blanket pulled tight and tucked in with hospital corners. Pillows were to be fluffed and stacked one on the other. Alison was not nearly as strict as the other housemothers, but she still had never been able to give any of the beds in 407 a checkmark.

"You know," she once told them, "in the Army they want those blankets so tight you can bounce a dime off them. I'm nowhere near that persnickety, but really — you couldn't bounce a trampolinist off any of *these* beds!"

This morning, Shelley was, as usual, the first to get up. Most mornings, she went down the hall, took her shower, and then came back and woke up Faith, who needed less time to get ready. Now, though, she just let Faith fend for herself. Shelley and Faith had not spoken yet and the atmosphere in 407 was as black as its walls.

Because Shelley didn't wake Faith, by the

time Faith did wake up, it was to Dana's alarm. Dana didn't have a nine o'clock class that term and so could sleep later. Her alarm went off at eight-thirty. This gave Faith half an hour to shower and dress and get over to Main Building for her biology class.

"Oh no!" she cried, when she realized what Shelley had done, and how late it had made her. Then she realized today was Room Check and moaned, "Double oh no!"

"Mmmmmrphmn?" Dana said, pulling her head up from the pillow.

"Shelley didn't wake me, naturally," Faith said. "And we've got Room Check this morning and we didn't clean last night and I've got to get out of here in about fifteen minutes. Can you process all this information?"

"Mmmmmrhmmm," Dana said. It sounded to Faith like what she had said before, but she was nodding as she said it and so Faith figured she was getting some level of comprehension. Faith went on. "This means you're going to have to clean by yourself today. I'll make it up to you next time, okay? Can you do that?"

Dana nodded again, but then dropped back down onto the pillow. Faith knelt by the side of her bed and gave it a shake. Dana opened one eye.

"Me Faith. Me late."

Dana kept her one eye open.

"Today Wednesday. Room Check. You clean."

"Okay," Dana said. "No problem."

Faith sighed with relief at finally getting her message across, and headed for the showers.

She forgot all about Room Check until that afternoon when she got back from classes. Taped to the door was a note from Alison. It said:

CONGRATULATIONS! YOU GOT AN 8. ALL-TIME BAKER LOW. THE AVERAGE *CAVE* COULD GET A NINE. YOU MUST'VE WORKED AT IT TO GET THE PLACE INTO SUCH A MESS. ALSO, NEED TO SEE DANA — IMPORTANT!

Faith pushed the door open to find the room exactly as she had left it this morning. No, it was worse. She could swear those soda cans hadn't been there on the window sill when she last looked, and that there hadn't been that pile of crumpled paper balls around Shelley's desk.

Dana had apparently just completely ignored her plea. Not only was the room a total mess, but Dana hadn't even made up her own bed. It was all rumpled and there was an open box of cookies in among the sheets and blanket.

"What's this!" It was Dana's voice behind Faith. She turned.

"You ought to know. I begged you to take care of this this morning. And look what I come back to," Faith snapped and shoved

Alison's note at her. Dana took it and read it over and looked back around the room in bewilderment.

"But I *did* clean it up," she said.

"Good job," Faith said sarcastically.

"No, I did. Really."

"Must've been that a stiff wind came up, a tornado maybe — and blew everything all around. Then shut the window on its way back out. Really, Dana, *grow up*. It's one thing to mess up. But it's ten times worse to not be able to admit it and say you're sorry."

"But I don't have anything to be sorry about. I cleaned this room, and someone un-cleaned it!" Dana shouted.

"Dana, this isn't some horror movie where spirits are moving the lamps and sofas. This is real life. Maybe you dreamed that you cleaned it. But the plain fact is that you didn't and we got an eight, and are sure to have to go before dorm board. I've got to say, I'm getting to like living in this room a lot less lately."

"You're not the only one," Dana said angrily. Then, distracted for a moment, she re-read the note. "What do you think Alison wants to see me about?"

"I don't know, babe, maybe she wants to give you dusting lessons. You sure could use them."

CHAPTER FIFTEEN

Dana went straight up to Alison's. It was no use trying any more to convince Faith that she *had* cleaned up the room. And if she hung around any longer, Shelley would be back from drama club and she'd have to try to explain to *her* that she had cleaned the room.

Alison had her own apartment on the top floor of Baker. She called it The Penthouse. It was Dana's dream apartment. In addition to having lots of big windows, it also had skylights in the living room and bedroom, so it was like living in a tree house.

Alison kept the old New England plank wood floors free of rugs. Instead, she had scattered around the living room floor a collection of big floor pillows. Three comfortable armchairs and a wall of bookcases made the room warm and homey. At the windows, she had natural cream-colored gauzy curtains that billowed in the slightest breeze.

Off the living room, she had a sun deck.
Out there in the warm weather, she had
arranged some old lawn furniture made out
of bent branches, that one of the school
janitors had found in the basement. She put
pale yellow cushions on them and set them
under an old beach umbrella. It looked like
someplace you'd find ladies in hoop skirts
sitting and fanning themselves and drinking
lemonade and eating little cucumber sand-
wiches with the crusts cut off.

Now though, when Alison opened the door
to Dana, Dana could see that the door to the
deck was shut against the new fall winds, and
that the yellow cushions had been brought
inside. This made Dana sad. She always
hated to see the last traces of summer.

"Hi," Dana said. "Please don't yell at me
about the room. I really *did* clean it, even if
no one believes me. Something funny's going
on down there. Shelley's mad at Faith for
writing a nasty letter Faith says she didn't
write. Faith's furious with Shelley for standing her up, when I know Shel was out on a
date with Tom that she'd had planned for
quite a few days. And now they're *both* going
to hate me for not cleaning a room I really
cleaned!"

Alison eyed her seriously and indicated
that she should come in. "Sit down. I just
made myself a pot of tea. I'll get you a cup."

She brought an old tea cup patterned all
over with roses, set it down on the floor in
front of Dana, and poured tea into it.

"The room's the least of your worries, Dana," she said. "You're in big trouble. You and Casey. I've asked her to come up, too."

There was a soft knock on the door. It was Casey.

"Tea party?" she said smiling, when she saw the pot and cups on the floor. Tea parties were one of Alison's specialties.

"Not this time," Alison said.

Neither of the girls had ever seen her so serious.

"Ms. Allardyce asked me to speak to you. Apparently she's found out that the two of you have been spying on her. She wants to see you both at her house at noon tomorrow."

"At her house?" Casey said. "Are you sure she didn't mean at her office in Main Building?"

"Positive," Alison said. "Her house."

"That's a first," Dana said, "a personal invitation to the headmistress's house. That must mean we've moved into the big time of rule-breaking."

But Alison wasn't going to have any more information pried out of her. "I think you'd just better wait until tomorrow," she said.

Dana and Casey felt pretty miserable coming back down the stairs.

"We are in deep, deep trouble, pal," Casey said. "I'm the trouble expert around here, and I know when it looks bad. At least they haven't called our families yet. They always tell you when they're doing that. I would not feel real terrific about them calling my parents and telling them I'd been spending my free time lying around under a shrub, listening to people's private conversations."

"Ohh," Dana said, pressing her hand to her forehead, as if she was getting a big headache. "My mother would die. She thinks I'm such a good kid."

"You *are* such a good kid. You're just a very curious kid," Casey consoled Dana.

"No. This goes beyond curiosity. This goes into the category of None of Our Business. Why did I think I had to know who that guy was? P.A. has a right to a private life that's private."

"You're just saying this now," Casey said, "because we got caught."

"No," Dana said. "I was already feeling sort of crummy about it. Now I'm just feeling *really* crummy."

They had arrived at the landing between the fifth and fourth floors. They were alone in the stairwell. It was a frequently used place for private talks.

"Sit down here a minute," Casey said, pulling Dana by the hand. "There's another issue here we've got to think about."

"What?"

"Who snitched on us?"

"Ah," Dana said. "I hadn't thought about that."

"Who knew?" Casey asked. "I didn't tell anyone."

"Shelley and Faith," Dana said. "They were in the room when I got back from P.A.'s that night. I was covered with mud from where we'd been lying on our stomachs by the porch. I could hardly get by without an explanation. I thought about telling them I'd taken up night parachuting, but somehow I didn't think that would go over. Besides, I almost always wind up telling them everything."

"But now there's so much trouble among the three of you," Casey said and gave Dana a look heavy with extra meaning.

"Case, don't even suggest that it was either of them. There's been trouble in 407 before and I suppose there'll be trouble again, but no matter how bad it gets, none of us would ever do something like that to each other. We wouldn't. That's all."

"Well," Casey said, with a look on her face that showed she was doing some inner calculating, "if I didn't tell anyone and you didn't tell anyone but Faith and Shelley and you're positive they didn't tell P.A., then someone *they* told did it."

Dana nodded in agreement.

"I'll go have a talk with them now. It's going to be hard since we're not on speaking terms, but I think this pushes that aside. I'll get to the bottom of this. I promise," she said and pushed open the door to the fourth floor hallway.

She didn't go straight to 407, though. She stopped off and sat on the floor of the broom closet for half an hour. She had some serious thinking to do before she talked to anyone.

When she walked back into the room half an hour later, both Faith and Shelley were there, studying at their desks, their backs to each other in symbolic hostility.

Dana stood in the doorway and cleared her throat. They both looked up at her. "We've got to talk," Dana said.

"Not interested," Shelley said, and went back to her book. Faith continued to look at Dana, but didn't say anything. It was as if she were waiting for further information.

"This is important. Really."

Shelley closed her book and said coldly, "What's it about?"

"Casey and I have been called on the carpet by P.A. She found out about the night we were skulking around, listening to her and The Guy."

"How'd she find out?" Faith asked.

"That's what we have to figure out," Dana said. "I know we haven't been the best of friends this week, but I also know that underneath everything, we still love each other and wouldn't hurt each other like this. What I think is that someone is sabotaging us."

"How?" Shelley asked, unconvinced.

"Someone's trying to undermine our faith in each other, to destroy our friendship with underhanded tricks," Dana said. "That letter Faith supposedly wrote, well, I've been thinking, and I'm sure Faith didn't write it. Read it again. It doesn't even sound like Faith. I've never heard her call Sarah, *Sis*. And whoever called you at the *Clarion*, Faith, it wasn't Shelley. She didn't know a thing about that call. That's why she never showed up. And unless I've gone completely off my rocker, I know when I've made a bed and cleaned a room, and that's what I did before I left here this morning. If it was messed up by the time we got back here, it's because someone messed it up on purpose. And my guess is that it's the same person who pulled the other nasty tricks. *And* the same person who told P.A. about me and Casey spying on her."

"Do you know who it is?" Faith asked.

Dana shook her head no. "We have to think hard and be honest about who each of us told about me and Casey. Casey says she didn't tell anyone and I believe her. Casey never tells anyone anything. That's why half the girls in school confide in her. I know I only told you two. No one else, and I know you didn't tell P.A. But whoever you did tell is the culprit."

For a long moment, no one said anything. Then Faith spoke up. "I didn't tell anyone. Not even Johnny. I wanted to tell him, but I didn't want to add to the risk you took. The way I figure, every person you tell about something, well it sort of geometrically ups the chances of someone spilling the beans."

There was another long moment of silence as Dana and Faith turned to Shelley and waited for her to say something. Finally she said, in a very small voice, "I told Pamela."

There was complete silence in the room,

and then Dana said, "Why? Didn't you know she'd do something awful?"

Faith just stared at Shelley. Then she asked in a low voice, "What was wrong, Shelley? That you would do something so thoughtless?"

Shelley reverted to the little girl, the way she often did when she was in trouble and distraught. She started to cry loudly and to try to talk as she wept.

"I don't *know* why I did it. I was angry at you, Faith, and I thought Dana had deliberately not cleaned the room and I felt like I had no friends, so I wanted Pamela to like me, even though I knew she was rotten, so to make me look important, to impress her, I told her about Dana and Casey, thinking I would seem like very *with it* just to know kids who would do something like eavesdrop on the headmistress. I do that a lot, I don't think before I take some kind of dumb action, I don't mean to be thoughtless or to hurt people, but I know that I do sometimes and then I can't stand myself."

Dana and Faith listened as Shelley went on. Finally, Dana said, but not without arfection, "Oh Shelley, shut up."

Shelley stopped talking in the middle of a sentence.

Faith sat down on the floor and started doing sit-ups. "This helps me think," she said as Shelley and Dana gazed at her in amazement.

"What we have to do," Faith said, panting

and puffing, "is stop ranting at Shelley, since what is done is done, but think about how we are going to get even with Old Pammy. We can't let her get away with all this meanness and rottenness."

"What can we do?" Shelley asked.

"Well," Faith said thoughtfully, "we can get her where it will bother her the most. Where is that?"

Dana said immediately, "It's in that big, inflated ego of hers."

"Right," Faith said. "And that is what we have to work on . . . a plan to collapse that inflated ego."

CHAPTER SIXTEEN

Dana met Casey in the cafeteria for breakfast the next day.

Casey was already there, stirring around something white and thick in a bowl on the table in front of her. Dana set her own tray down and asked, "What're you eating?"

"Cream of paste," Casey said. "I'm not eating it. I'm just stirring it. So what happened after we split last night?"

Dana sat down and took a sip of coffee and a bite of toast and chewed and swallowed and said. "Well, we've got a culprit."

"Who?"

"Pamela the Wonderful. We're pretty sure she's the one who pulled all those stunts this week. Why, I don't know."

"An all-round great gal," Casey said sarcastically. "So what're you going to do — put her in the old Puritan stocks in the town square in Greenleaf?"

Dana smiled slowly. "Oh, we've got a better plan than that. I'll tell you all about it later. Right now we've got to think about what we're going to say when P.A. gets us on the grill."

"We could lie," Casey said. "It's probably just Pamela's word against ours."

Dana thought for a minute. "I guess we could. It would probably be the easiest way out. But I don't want to do that. I'm feeling bad enough for having spied. I'd hate to add lying to spying." Then she giggled a little when she realized she was rhyming.

"I'm for telling the truth, too," Casey said. "The time I got called on the carpet by P.A. a year ago, after I started to run away, she was really pretty decent to me. I owe her one."

"But what defense can we come up with?" Dana wondered, idly poking at her sunnyside yolk with a corner of her toast.

"We could say the *Clarion* asked us to do an exposé of her," Casey offered.

"We could say we were practicing for the soon-to-be-formed Canby Hall Night Crawling team," Dana said.

"We could say one of us lost her contact and we were scouring the campus for it," Casey said.

"We could say the food has gotten so bad that we were out on her lawn *grazing*," Dana said.

But at the end of all this joking, they knew they weren't going to cook up any phony defense.

"I think all we can do is throw ourselves on P.A.'s mercy," Dana said.

Both girls grew glum. They were thinking the same thing. Casey was the first to say it out loud. "Mercy is not P.A.'s strong suit."

Dana nodded.

"Of course, like I said, she was pretty fair to me last year," Casey remembered.

"Yes," Dana said, "but you weren't being bad that time. Not really. You were upset and in trouble. That's different. Think how P.A. treats most rule-breakers. And they're just girls who've offended the school rules. We've offended P.A. *personally*! This is not going to be fun. I wouldn't be surprised if she's down in her basement right now — dusting the cobwebs out of the dungeon."

Most days by noon, Dana was starving. Today though, she couldn't have eaten lunch on a bet. She walked from her Spanish class over to the headmistress's house with the slowest, smallest steps imaginable. Casey was waiting for her by the huge oak tree in front of the house.

In spite of their nervousness, they burst out laughing when they saw each other. Both of them had changed into their sweetest dresses and pastel sweaters.

"Why if it isn't Little Miss Goody Two Shoes," Dana said, curtsying.

"And my old friend Pollyanna," Casey replied, returning the curtsy.

"Who do we think we're kidding?" Dana

said. "P.A. is going to see through these outfits in a second. What time is it? I forgot my watch."

"Two minutes till," Casey said, looking at her wristwatch.

"Well," Dana said with a large sigh, "I guess we'd better go and face the music. I don't think it would go over too well to be late to this."

When they got up on the wide front porch, the two of them stood for a long moment in front of the door, neither wanting to ring the bell.

Finally, Dana reached out and pressed the button and they heard a jangly ringing on the other side of the door. Almost immediately, as if she'd been standing with her hand on the knob, the door was opened by Mrs. Benbow, Patrice Allardyce's housekeeper.

Mrs. Benbow was a stern woman with steel gray hair, a tight set to her jaw, and a suspicious look in her eye. The rumor was that Mrs. Benbow was a dark force lurking around the headmistress's house. It was said that she put lemon juice in Ms. Allardyce's tea every morning to sour her disposition. And that she filled Patrice Allardyce's head with suspicions about Canby girls, and egged her on to give stiffer punishments for rule-breaking. Dana didn't know whether or not to believe this stuff. She thought there was an equally good chance that Mrs. Benbow's expression and manner were the results of a bad back or bunions, and that she could care less what was going on around school.

Still, she had to admit that when Mrs. Benbow opened the door and peered at them through squinting eyes and said, "Yesssss?" that she *was* looking at them pretty suspiciously — as if they were, at any minute, about to turn from innocent schoolgirls into armed robbers.

"We have an appointment to see Ms. Allardyce," Dana said, trying to sound confident, as if they were the co-chairpersons of the Christmas Ball decorations committee or something like that, and this visit were a business call.

"Oh, the two little sneaking spies," Mrs. Benbow said, looking at them as if they were worms that had crawled out onto the porch after last night's rain. "Come in then. Ms. Allardyce is expecting you."

They followed her into a large front hall that smelled of wood and polish and flowers. There was a vase of roses on the hall table.

"This way," Mrs. Benbow said sharply, leading them through a wide doorway into a study. "Ms. Allardyce will be with you presently," she said, then left the room, shutting the door behind her.

Dana and Casey looked around at the book-lined walls, the flowered chintz-covered sofa, the big walnut desk, and the French doors leading out onto the side garden. They were nervous at being in a room they had expected

to be imposing that had turned out instead
to be comfortable.

"Should we just stand here, or sit down, or
what?" Dana asked.

"I don't know," Casey said. "I guess sit."
She nodded toward two armchairs set in front
of the desk. "Those look like the hot seats."

They sat down and smoothed the skirts of
their dresses over their knees, positioned their
feet close together on the carpet, and folded
their hands in their laps.

Patrice Allardyce came in so quietly behind
them that they didn't know she was in the
room until she said, "Ah, such little ladies.
Such models of decorum. Such perfect repre-
sentatives of the spirit of Canby Hall." Ms.
Allardyce was a pro at sarcasm.

She sat down in the large, high-backed
chair behind the desk. She leaned forward
slightly, put her arms on the surface of the
desk, clasped her hands, and looked hard at
each of them in turn, then she said, "All right.
Why don't you tell me why you did it."

Dana didn't want Casey to take the re-
sponsibility.

"It was my idea," she said. "Casey was just
an accomplice. My curiosity just ran away
with me is all. After I saw you and — your
friend — out at Lovers' Leap that morning, I
just had to find out more."

"And what did you find out by crawling
around that night?"

"Oh," Dana said, trying to think fast. "Not

much. I guess we weren't around long enough to hear anything very interesting."

Patrice Allardyce didn't say anything. She just continued to sit and look directly at Dana and wait. She didn't come out and say she didn't believe Dana. She just sat and waited for her to come up with the truth.

"Well," Dana said nervously after a while of being patiently stared at, "we heard a little something about him being in prison."

The headmistress continued to remain silent.

"And about your waiting," Dana blurted out. "That kind of stuff."

"Very personal, private stuff," Ms. Allardyce said.

"Yes ma'am."

Patrice Allardyce took a long time before she spoke again. "The thing that bothers me most is that you girls think it's cute when you do something like this. Schoolgirl hijinks. Harmless fun. But if the tables were turned — if I came by at night and hung around eavesdropping on your conversations, you'd be outraged at the invasion."

Dana had to admit that she was right. Teachers or housemothers or the headmistress spying on the students seemed too creepy for words. And so her syping was just as creepy. At least from what Ms. Allardyce said, she didn't know the part about the telescope. For some reason, Dana felt worst about that part, although by now she was feeling terrible about the whole thing.

"I don't have any good defense," Dana said in a soft voice. "I wish I did. All I can say is that I really am sorry. I do try to be sensitive to other people's feelings. I just fall short sometimes. I guess you seem so far above the rest of us, it didn't occur to me that you would be affected by something *I* did."

Patrice Allardyce nodded, then looked over at Casey.

"I guess I just wasn't thinking at all," Casey said. "That sometimes happens. I'm sorry, too. Really. And not just because we got caught."

"I'm glad you're both sorry. And I believe you. Sometimes we have to make mistakes to see that they are mistakes. The fact remains, though, that this was a serious violation of both morality and manners. And so the punishment will have to be rather severe. I'm going to restrict you both to campus for the next month."

Dana and Casey swallowed their groans.

"You know, all of this unpleasantness could have been avoided if you had only come directly to me expressing your interest in meeting Yale. He's here now." She picked up the receiver on the intercom phone on her desk. "Mrs. Benbow? Could you find Yale and send him down to the study? Thank you."

The three of them waited in silence for the few minutes it took for the knock to come on the door.

"Come in," Ms. Allardyce shouted out lightly.

The door opened and in walked The Guy.

He had on jeans and a t-shirt streaked with grease. He smiled across the room at Ms. Allardyce and said, "I think I've got that carburetor of yours working again." Then he noticed Dana and Casey.

"Yale, I'd like you to meet two students who are very interested in your presence here."

He nodded politely and smiled.

"Dana Morrison and Casey Flint, I'd like you to meet Yale Allardyce. My brother."

CHAPTER SEVENTEEN

Although the calendar had flipped a page, over into October, one day was a reprieve — sunny and warm with puffy, drifting clouds. Dana and Alison were taking advantage of this last shot of summer. They had put the cushions back on the ancient lawn furniture and were sitting out on Alison's deck, sipping tea and eating some of the carrot cake Dana's mother had sent up from New York.

"Why couldn't you have told me he was her brother?" Dana was saying. "Saved me a month's grounding."

"I couldn't," Alison said. "When Yale first turned up here, Patrice was quite unsettled. They were very close in childhood. But then he started getting into trouble . . . suspended from two schools, drunk, petty thefts. She was terribly disappointed in him and hurt.

Then when he stole a car and got sent to prison, she felt he had betrayed himself and her. After their parents had died, she had devoted herself to raising him. She was very angry. Plus she knew it wouldn't do her a lot of good with the board of trustees and parents, if it were known that her brother was in the clink. And so she shut him out of her life. Pretended she didn't have a brother."

"But even after he got out?" Dana said.

"She was still angry and upset. She didn't know for sure if he had changed. He was still hurt. They had a lot of things to settle between them. The kind of things you and Casey overheard that night, I guess. But now he's convinced her that he's gone straight. He's got a good mechanic's job over at Hanson's Garage in town. I hear she's planning to introduce him to everyone at the Harvest Holiday dance next week, so it's okay to tell you all this now. Sorry I couldn't before, but I was respecting Patrice's right to privacy."

"Which is more than I did," Dana said dejectedly.

"Well, it wasn't your finest hour," Alison admitted. "But we all do dumb things now and then. I think I can still stand to be your friend," Alison teased. Dana lunged over to tickle her housemother.

"You're going to make me drop my cake," Alison shouted between fits of laughter.

Suddenly Dana stopped. "I just remembered," she said. "I've got to be somewhere now."

Alison peered at her. "Do I detect a little mystery here?" she said.

"Well, Shelley and Faith and Casey and I have a piece of unfinished business to take care of with Pamela Young."

Alison nodded.

"It's tough to know sometimes where to stop being a housemother and start being a person. I mean, I suppose technically, I should tell you not to get back at Pamela. But my heart wouldn't be in it. Just try to stay away from the truly grisly, will you? I mean, don't drop her in a pool of quicksand or feed her to a Venus flytrap or anything like that."

"Don't worry. What we have in mind isn't even very nasty. Just creative. We just need to teach Pamela some manners."

CHAPTER EIGHTEEN

By the time Dana got back down to 407, the other three had already put into gear the first phase of Plan DPC — Drive Pamela Crazy.

"Where've you been?" Shelley asked Dana.

"Sorry. I got lost in space up at Alison's. Did you send the note?"

"I put it by her door," Casey said. "I've got study hall last period so I could do it while she was still in class. I added my own little special touch, too."

"What?" Dana asked.

"I attached it to a long-stemmed red rose. Brilliant, eh?"

"What'd the note say exactly?" Dana said.

"Here's a copy," Faith said, handing Dana a piece of lined notebook paper. On it was typed:

Darling,
Sorry I haven't been around too much lately. It's just that I've been scared.

You're so intoxicating, so magnetic that
I was afraid of falling *too* hard. But I
can't stay away any longer. I have to see
you. Please meet me at the Auberge for
tea this afternoon at four. I have many
things I want to whisper in your ear.

Love,
Bret

"Whew," Dana said, waving the note
through the air as if it were too hot to handle.
"But how can you be sure he hasn't been
calling her lately?"

"He and Natalie Fenton have been the
hottest item on campus for a couple of weeks
now. Pamela must have gotten wind of it,"
Faith said. "Even if she didn't care much
about him, she probably cares plenty that
everyone knows she got dumped. As we all
know, Pamela has the giant economy size
ego. And so she's bound to go for this bait."

Shelley started rubbing her hands together
and dancing around like a cartoon character
up to lots of mischief. The others took her
lead and started in themselves, giggling and
grinning all the while.

"What time is it?" Casey asked. "We don't
want to miss our cue."

"Quarter after four," Shelley said, glancing
at the clock on the window sill.

"Let's give her another five minutes or so
to get kind of edgy," Faith said.

Shelley called Tom and told him. "Wait
until twenty after, then call the Auberge,

pretend you're Bret, and leave a message with the maitre d'. Tell him to tell Pamela that you got detention and won't be out until five. You'll meet her under the big clock at Main Building at five after."

Dana, Faith, Shelley, and Casey sat in an empty classroom across from Main Building, looking out the window at the big clock across the way. The big clock was a traditional meeting place for Canby girls and Oakley boys.

But the four of them had their eye on one particular boy — Ed Merritt, who was Tom's best friend. What he was doing down there now, though, hanging around the base of the clock, was pretending to be Bret Harper's best friend.

The girls had enlisted Ed as someone Pamela didn't know, who could say he was relaying a message from Bret. They'd given Ed a detailed description of Pamela, so he would know who to look for, although even a sketchy description would probably have been enough. There wasn't anybody around Canby Hall who looked remotely like Pamela, except Pamela.

"*Here's* Pammy!" Faith said, imitating Ed McMahon.

"Where?" Dana said.

"See," Faith said, "coming down the path from the Science Building?"

"Oh yeah. I see her. Holding her rose. Isn't that cute? She's walking pretty slowly, though, for someone who's supposed to be excited to meet her boyfriend."

"You forget," Casey said, "that Pamela is always cool. She'd never let any guy know she was on pins and needles. That walk is calculated down to the millisecond."

"Oh good," Shelley said, "Ed's spotted her. He's going over. He's introducing himself."

"Shelley," Faith said patiently. "We are all — as you may notice — looking out the same window. This is not a foreign film. We don't need subtitles."

"Okay, I'll shut up. I won't bother you with *exactly* what it is Ed's telling Pamela right now. I won't tell you the really gooey romantic message *I* cooked up for him to pass along. I don't want to *bore* anyone with details."

"Ooops," Faith said. "Sorry I cut you off, girl."

"How sorry?" Shelley teased.

Faith dropped to her knees and took Shelley's hand.

"Okay. I guess I can try to remember my exact wording," Shelley said as Faith got up. "I believe Ed is at this very moment telling Pamela that Bret thought twice about meeting her someplace as ordinary as the clock. He wants her to meet him out by the big tree near the skating pond, where he can give her his romantic surprise with the proper amount of privacy; where it can be just the two of them; where they can pretend they're the only two people in the world."

"I don't know why," Faith said sarcastically, "but I'm having a real hard time imagining Ed Merritt — Mr. Pacman — speaking those words to a girl."

"Well," Shelley admitted, "he did seem sort of reluctant to go that far. The way he put it was that he was afraid to make a speech that long, that one of the rubber bands on his braces was bound to spring out."

"Wait," Faith said. "It looks like there's some hitch. Pamela looks teed off."

"Uh-oh," Dana said. "We should've got someone more persuasive than good old Ed. Or else we should've given him twice as many quarters as we did. Enough so he could rush off and really drown his nervousness in a couple of hours of Pacman."

"Wait," Casey said. "I think things are back on track. Pamela's shrugging her shoulders. Like a sigh. She's looking at her watch. That must mean she's going to go for it. Come on gang! We've got to get out to the skating pond before her!"

The four of them raced down the back stairs of Baker and out into the woods behind the dorm. They took the wooded paths the long way around the perimeter of the campus so they wouldn't run into Pamela along the way. Figuring that Pamela would saunter over to the pond at her ultracool pace, they would have at least a five to ten minute leap on her. Plenty of time to set everything up.

* * *

"Okay," Dana said when they all got there. "Who's got the blanket?"

"Me," Shelley said. "Here. Help me spread it out nicely here under the tree. Now, where are the candles?"

Casey pulled them out of her knapsack.

"Here," she said. "But how are we going to keep them lit outside?"

"It doesn't matter if they stay lit," Faith said. "It's the sentiment that counts. Now here. Here's the crepe paper. I got pink and blue. Boy and girl. Isn't it sweet. Almost makes me want to cry."

From there, they added the finishing touches — a vase of freshly-picked wild-flowers, a portable radio playing the most romantic music they could tune in to. The crepe paper hung in long loops from the branches of the tree, and on the trunk, they tacked red construction paper hearts with BRET & PAMELA printed on them. There was everything Pamela could ask for — except, of course, for Bret.

When they were done, they took off through the woods, over to Old Fort Road, in the opposite direction from the way Pamela would be coming.

They waited there for twenty minutes or so.

"Do you think she's there yet?" Shelley asked.

"Oh sure," Dana said, looking at her watch.

"I figure she's probably been there ten minutes at least. We probably ought to start back now."

"Get out that bird book, Casey," Faith said, pulling a pair of binoculars from her backpack. "The first meeting of the Baker House Birdwatching Society is about to come to order."

They set out walking and, when they'd come almost back to the romantic setting, they started talking among themselves about robins and blue jays and hummingbirds.

"Here!" Dana shouted, leading them into the clearing where Pamela would be sitting, "I think I saw a thrush!" They all followed her.

And all simultaneously pretended to be quite surprised to find Pamela sitting there. Everyone was quiet for a long moment.

Shelley broke the silence with a, "Hi, Pamela." She was careful not to make it too friendly lest Pamela smell a rat.

"Hi, Shelley," Pamela said, then nodded around at the others by way of general greeting, then flushed bright red under her fading tan when she realized what a goon she looked like sitting all by herself in this outrageously romantic set-up.

"You expecting someone?" Dana asked her, with as much innocence as she could get into her voice.

"Oh, well sure," she said, then waved her hand at all the decorations. "I didn't *do* this, you understand. It's a surprise *for* me. Dear

Bretto. Such a hopeless romantic. If you don't mind, I'm going to ask you all to clear out now. I'm expecting him any second now and we won't be needing any company. I wonder where he could be?"

"Well," Faith said, "as of ten minutes ago, he was strolling across campus, hand in hand with Natalie Fenton. We saw them on the way out here."

Pamela glared at Faith, then at the others in turn.

"I don't believe you," she said in a voice so haughty that it was clear she didn't.

"Suit yourself," Faith said, then turned to the others. "Well, we'd better run along if we're going to spot us a raven before it gets too dark." She turned back to Pamela. "See you around."

Nobody said anything until they were well out of Pamela's earshot.

"How long do you think she'll sit there?" Shelley asked the others when they were back in the main part of campus.

"A while," Faith said. "First she has to give up on Bret. Then she's got to wait a while after that to make sure she doesn't run into us."

"I don't think she's caught on yet," Casey said.

"No," Dana said, "But she will fast, as soon as she calls poor old Bret — excuse me, Dear Bretto — to read him the riot act, and he doesn't know what on earth she's talking about!"

As they walked into 407, Shelley said, "She'll be down here to read *us* the riot act. She'll know we set her up."

"I can hardly wait," Dana said.

The girls tried to keep busy as they waited for Pamela. Shelley experimented painting her nails two tone; half of each nail bright red and half pink. Dana tried to jog in place, and Faith just paced, muttering as she did . . . "That crummy girl."

Finally, the door burst open and Pamela walked in. Her usually pale face was flushed and she was out of breath, as if she had finally walked, *ran*, someplace.

"You three did it. Didn't you? You planned the whole thing."

"Aren't we clever?" Shelley asked.

Pamela turned on Shelley and her face twisted up. "You . . . of all people. After all I did for you, making a little Iowa hick my friend."

Shelley started for Pamela, but Faith grabbed her. "Nothing physical, girl."

Shelley drew herself up as tall as she could, and put on her total stage personality. "I'll ignore your *childish* remarks about my *birthplace*, but don't you *dare* call yourself a friend. As soon as my back was turned, you tried to steal my boyfriend. *That* is low."

Pamela turned to Dana. "Why did you do this? What do you have against me, outside of being jealous because *you* were no longer Miss Chic when I arrived?"

Dana laughed out loud. "What did we have against you? How stupid can you be? Or more important, how stupid do you think *we* are? You planted that letter in Faith's typewriter, knowing we would see it and you hoped we'd believe she really wrote it. Then you sent Faith on a wild goose chase, making her think Shelley wanted to meet her. And *then* you messed up our room, after I almost killed myself cleaning it. And *then* you reported that Casey and I spied on P.A. And you ask what we have against you?"

"What don't we?" Faith said. "Why did you do all that awful stuff? What have *you* got against *us*?"

Pamela paced around the room in a rage. "You three. You think you're so special. That you have the perfect friendship. You're always together, always so comfy and close. You keep everyone else out of your little, exclusive circle. I thought it would be fun to see how much you really care about each other. I almost did it though. Right? I almost split you up."

"Almost doesn't count," Faith said. "And what you said isn't true. We have lots of other friends and we don't keep people out. We just keep *some* people out."

"You almost had me fooled," Shelley said. "I almost thought you were trying to be a decent person."

Pamela laughed meanly and walked to the door. "Well, the year is just beginning. And I have a lot of other tricks up my sleeve. I'm not through with you three yet."

She left the room, slamming the door so hard that the walls shook.

"I don't know about you two," Faith said sarcastically, "but I'm *really* scared."

Dana looked serious, and said, "She was right, though. She *did* come close to breaking us up. Too close."

The three of them thought about this for a moment, then Shelley brightened.

"But she didn't," she said, taking both her roommates by the hand.

"And she's not going to," Faith declared.

"More power to us," Dana said with conviction. "We're still together. Still best friends forever."